CURSED WEB

MOONSHADOW BAY
BOOK 9

YASMINE GALENORN

A Nightqueen Enterprises LLC Publication

Published by Yasmine Galenorn

PO Box 2037, Kirkland WA 98083-2037

CURSED WEB

A Moonshadow Bay Novel

Copyright © 2023 by Yasmine Galenorn

First Electronic Printing: 2023 Nightqueen Enterprises LLC

First Print Edition: 2023 Nightqueen Enterprises

Cover Art & Design: Ravven

Art Copyright: Yasmine Galenorn

Editor: Elizabeth Flynn

ALL RIGHTS RESERVED No part of this book may be reproduced or distributed in any format, be it print or electronic or audio, without permission. Please prevent piracy by purchasing only authorized versions of this book.

This is a work of fiction. Any resemblance to actual persons, living or dead, businesses, or places is entirely coincidental and not to be construed as representative or an endorsement of any living/ existing group, person, place, or business.

A Nightqueen Enterprises LLC Publication

Published in the United States of America

ACKNOWLEDGMENTS

Welcome back to January Jaxson's world—the world of Moonshadow Bay.

Thanks to my usual crew: Samwise, my husband, Andria and Jennifer—without their help, I'd be swamped. To the women who have helped me find my way in indie, you're all great, and thank you to everyone. To my wonderful cover artist, Ravven, for the beautiful work she's done. Thanks to my best friend Carol Shannon, one of the most remarkable and magickal women I know.

Also, my love to my furbles, who keep me happy. My heart is over the rainbow with my Rainbow Girls, and here in the present with our current babies. My most reverent devotion to Mielikki, Tapio, Ukko, Rauni, and Brighid, my spiritual guardians and guides. My love and reverence to Herne, and Cernunnos, and to the Fae, who still rule the wild places of this world. And a nod to the Wild Hunt, which runs deep in my magick, as well as in my fiction.

You can find me through my website at **Galenorn.com** and be sure to sign up for my **newsletter** to keep updated on all my latest releases and to access the VIP section of my website, which has all sorts of perks on it! You can find my advice on writing, discussions about the books, and general ramblings on my YouTube Channel and my blog. If you liked this book, I'd be grateful if you'd leave a review—it helps more than you can think.

Brightest Blessings,

-The Painted Panther-
-Yasmine Galenorn-

WELCOME TO CURSED WEB

Now that I know where Gretchen Wyre lives—the witch who hexed my great-great-grandmother and all her female descendants—it's time to break the curse. I enlist my grandmother Rowan and my grandmother Naomi—who's visiting from Ireland—to help. But just because we know where Gretchen is doesn't guarantee success. And some curses take on a demonic life of their own, and those demons aren't willing to vanish into the sunset without a fight.

Reading Order for the Moonshadow Bay Series:

- Book 1: Starlight Web
- Book 2: Midnight Web
- Book 3: Conjure Web
- Book 4: Harvest Web
- Book 5: Shadow Web
- Book 6: Weaver's Web
- Book 7: Crystal Web
- Book 8: Witch's Web
- Book 9: Cursed Web
- Book 10: Solstice Web (forthcoming)

CHAPTER ONE

We were nearing Samhain—the festival of the ancestors—and the Veil was thin. I could feel it in my bones. I could sense it in the air. Autumn had come in with a vengeance and everywhere I looked, ghosts were walking. It wasn't that there were more of them than usual, but my perception was growing and it was driving me nuts. I wanted to focus on something other than death, especially with my wedding coming up in a couple of months. At least I had Nonny's visit to look forward to.

"I can't believe I'm going to see Nonny! I haven't seen her since I was a little girl, even though we've talked. I hope…" I stopped, faltering.

"You hope what?" Killian asked.

We were sitting on the bed, talking. My grandmother Naomi was due in tomorrow, and we were slated to drive over to Bellingham International Airport to pick her up. It would be the first time I'd seen her since I was eight. We'd kept in touch, but face to face? That had been thirty-four years ago.

"I hope she's proud of me." I adjusted my wrap top over

my jeans. It was low cut, a gorgeous cobalt blue, and it fit my curves nicely. "My parents are dead, and Aunt Teran loves me no matter what. But Nonny's no-nonsense. She doesn't put up with any bullshit or slackers."

"From what she sounds like on the phone, I don't think you have to worry about that," Killian said. "Are you ready? We're due at our appointment with Carrie in twenty minutes."

Carrie Oshner ran Carrie's Bakery & Wedding Cakes, one of the best bakeries in town. She was as skilled with a piping bag as Monet had been with a paintbrush. And we had an eleven-thirty appointment with her to discuss our wedding cake. We had originally planned to go with Sirus Barker, who owned Violet's Tea Dreams Shop—a tea shop he named after his wife—but he and Violet had decided on a trip to Europe, and they would be gone during our wedding. He had recommended Carrie to us with glowing reviews.

So far we had booked the venue—we were getting married at Mulberry Farm's Clydesdale Mansion. London Mulberry, a local heiress, owned a hundred acres on the outskirts of town. There were several venues for rent there, including the most prominent setting—the Clydesdale Mansion, which was on a ten-acre patch of land. With a large hall, ten bedroom suites, two large main bathrooms, a kitchen, and a spacious garden, it was the perfect place for a winter wedding. If it was raining or snowing, we'd get married in the hall. If it was clear and not too cold, we were planning an outdoor ceremony in the main gazebo. Either way, the venue was perfect.

I was still debating on whether to wear my dress. I'd unknowingly bought a haunted wedding dress that had belonged to a bride murdered by a demon. While I loved the dress and had broken the curse holding her spirit to it, every time I looked at it, I shivered. The thought of wearing a murder-dress, as I'd taken to calling it, bothered me more and more as the autumn deepened. I didn't have much time to find a new one, but since I wasn't planning on a traditional wedding dress, I figured the odds were with me, especially since we were headed into the holiday season when fancy clothes abounded.

Other than the dress and venue, we'd locked my grandmother Rowan into officiating. As the high priestess of the Crystal Cauldron coven, she couldn't very well say no. We'd also taken care of the invitations and booked a caterer, and the wedding cake was the biggest decision we had left to make.

I touched up my makeup and grabbed my purse, making sure my keys were inside. Killian was driving but I never left home without keys and phone.

Xi and Klaus were sprawled out across the bed, napping. No longer kittens but still playful, they had graduated to the point where they spent a lot of their time asleep.

My gorgeous tortie and I were growing closer. Xi was growing in her power, but I wasn't pushing her. Familiars evolved at their own pace and there was absolutely nothing you could do to speed up their development. I loved my cats like some people loved their children, but Xi and I had a special connection and now and then, when I had bad dreams, she would show up in them to protect me. Klaus seemed absolutely content with his lot in life. While he couldn't talk to me the way Xi could, he was happy and healthy, and that was all that mattered.

At Carrie's, we spent half an hour discussing the wedding cake and tasting samples. She had ten choices, with everything from chocolate hazelnut to honey vanilla to gingerbread to carrot cake. But Killian and I both knew what we wanted and we agreed on a three-tier dark chocolate cake with raspberry filling and Swiss meringue buttercream. Carrie would cover the cake in white fondant, wrap each tier around the bottom with a blue ribbon, and then cascade a curtain of blue roses down the sides. The design was beautiful, elegant, and magical.

Carrie boxed up the rest of the samples for us. I wanted to pay for them but she shook her head. "I'd just throw them away. I always make new samples for each client. And since you've already given me a deposit on the cake, you might as well take these home and enjoy them."

It occurred to me that since we'd put down a non-refundable deposit, we might as well accept them. The cake was costing us six hundred and change.

"They'll be gone in a couple days. Trust me," I said, staring at the ten mini-cakes that were half-intact. Each sampler equaled about four cupcakes. Which meant we had about thirty cupcakes worth of dessert left. *Really good* dessert.

As we were leaving the shop, Killian's phone rang. I took the bags from him while he answered.

"Hello?" At first he looked puzzled, but then he stopped in the middle of the sidewalk and the smile slid off his face. "*What?* When did this happen?" His voice dipped and he caught his breath. "When?... Yes, I can make it. Where's the funeral going to be held?"

Funeral?

Praying it wasn't someone in his family, I watched the sky. The clouds were socking in, dark and heavy with rain. We were due for a windstorm, and I still had chores to finish in order to prepare for it. Western Washington had wild storms almost every November, and sometimes they came as early as October. High winds and heavy downpours led to trees crashing down, power outages, landslides, and urban flooding.

"Listen, Ken, can you text me the details? This is a lot to take in... Thanks, I appreciate it... Yeah, it's going to be odd without him. I agree with you on that." Killian pocketed his phone and reached for the bags. "Come on," he said. "I don't want to get soaked."

I wanted to ask him who had died, but he seemed lost in thought. I wasn't sure if it was grief or just shock, but whoever the news was about, it was obvious that it wasn't some stranger or mere acquaintance. I handed him the bags and we returned to the car in silence.

On the way home, Killian finally spoke. "That was Ken. Remember I told you I used to go camping with a group of guys in California?"

"Yeah, I remember."

"Well, Darby was...you might call him a frenemy. We got along for a long time, but then things changed. He was jealous of everybody about something. He wasn't a bad-looking fellow, but he didn't have a personality that attracted women. He was moody and passive. And then he blamed the women for not noticing him. He wasn't exactly an incel, but he never had a second date with anybody."

"And he was jealous of you because...?"

"He had a thing for a woman who had a crush on me. She made it abundantly clear that she was interested in me. I never asked her out because of the code. You know—you don't date someone your friend is interested in, unless there's an unavoidable chemistry there. And even then, you talk to your buddy first."

I nodded. "My friends and I all had the same code, too."

"Right. And I wasn't interested in her. She was nice, but she wasn't my type. But all Darby could see was that she wanted me and not him. He pretended that everything was all right, but I knew it wasn't. After that, Darby started taking potshots at me. It was obvious that he was still bitter. It's really a shame because he started out a good guy, but he ended up drinking too much and then, shortly before I moved up here, Darby ended up hooked on apnaeads—a similar drug to opioids for the shifter community. He got... twitchy. I wish I would have said something. Tried to get him into a facility, or something like that."

"You can't make somebody do something unless they're ready." I hesitated, then asked the question to which I already knew the answer. "How did he die?"

"He overdosed four days ago. His folks live here in Moonshadow Bay, actually. So they've shipped his body back here to be buried. The funeral is tonight. I know it's short notice, but do you mind if I bail on dinner tonight?"

I got the impression that he really didn't want to attend, but I also knew that he needed to say good-bye. Given his comment about wishing he could have helped Darby, I suspected Killian might be feeling some sort of survivor's guilt. Or maybe he was just in shock. Either way, the funeral would probably be difficult, but my guess was that it would help in the long run.

"Better than that, I'm coming with you. I'm your fiancée, and we help each other like this." Although I kept my thoughts to myself, it occurred to me that I might be able to sense whether Darby's spirit was hanging around the funeral home. If so, there would be a chance I could talk to him and find some closure for both him and Killian.

Killian glanced at me as he pulled into the driveway. "Are you sure? You never met him."

"I didn't have to meet him. He was part of your life, and it sounds like he was a complicated part of your life. And our lives are joined together now so what affects you, affects me. Just ask his parents if you can bring your fiancée, so that they don't feel awkward with me showing up unannounced." I slid out of the SUV and darted up the stairs to unlock the door as the rain began to pour down. Killian followed me carrying the sample cakes.

"Darby's folks don't mind if you come to the funeral with me," Killian said, peeking inside the kitchen where I was making dinner. "They sound grateful that anybody wants to come at all, which is sad."

"Yeah, that is sad," I said, staring into the fridge. "Do you want to eat before or after? We have an hour before we should leave."

"Let's have a snack before, and then we'll pick up a pizza on the way home. Or chicken. Whatever you want." Killian paused, then added, "Are you sure about this, January? I don't want you to feel obligated. Darby and I haven't really been friends for years. I'm going because I want to pay my respects to his family, not because I considered him a good buddy." He wrapped his arms around my waist and leaned over my shoulder.

I was chopping tomatoes, onion, and basil for the slow cooker. After mincing chives and tossing in some pepper, thyme, and oregano, I added sausage that I had precooked, drained, and crumbled, and turned the slow cooker to low. I was making sauce for tomorrow night's spaghetti dinner. Nonny would be here by then, and she always talked about spaghetti being her favorite during our email chats.

"Yes, I'm sure. As long as *you* don't mind me going. Now, make yourself useful and put the vegetable peelings in the compost bucket, if you would." I washed my hands, then began washing the counter with a soapy sponge.

"When does Nonny get here?" Killian asked. "And is Teran coming over tomorrow? Given that Nonny's her mother."

"Yeah, Teran's coming over in the morning, although I know they have a strained relationship. I'm not sure what happened, but every time Teran talks about her, I sense the tension. Nonny should be here by four PM, so we need to be at the airport by then." I finished stirring the sauce and settled the lid on it. "There. The sauce will be done by the time we get home, I think. It should be safe. The slow cooker is new. Tomorrow morning, we need to finish making up the guestroom."

"I'll help. I promise." Killian had volunteered to clean the guestroom and put new sheets on the bed. While he did that, I would clean the bathroom and tidy up the house.

To be honest, I was nervous about Nonny's visit. It had been so long since I had last seen her, and while we had talked throughout the years, there was a big difference in seeing someone in person. And Nonny was stern, sometimes scary stern.

I was putting the last of the dishes in the dishwasher when a flash of lightning lit up the sky. The lights flickered and I shivered as the rumble of thunder echoed through the night.

"I hope the storm doesn't get too bad. At least not till we get home." I wiped my hands on a tea towel, untied my apron, and glanced at the clock. "We should change clothes."

As we dressed, I asked Killian about his sister.

"Have you heard from Tally lately?"

Killian's sister had finally had her twins in July, and we had been spending a lot of time over at her house. We babysat to give Tally and Les time off. Little Victoria and Leanna were adorable. They hadn't shifted yet—that wouldn't come until they began to walk—but their eyes shimmered like Killian's when he was about to shift, and they had the aura of wolf shifters.

Killian was good with the babies and, as long as he pulled diaper duty, I was fine with watching them. But babysitting had definitely reinforced my realization that I wasn't cut out for motherhood, and even Killian mentioned how exhausting taking care of them was.

He had the patience of a saint, but then again, he worked with animals on a regular basis and that helped. By the end of our babysitting jaunts we were always relieved to head home. But we wanted to help out. We loved Tally, and Les was a nice guy, and while one baby was hard, two babies were double the trouble. So we gave them time away when we could.

"Actually, yes. Apparently my mother decided to show up on her doorstep the other day and she's staying for a month to help out. Since my father is on a road trip with his buddies, Mom took a leave of absence from work for a few weeks and is immersing herself in being a grandmama. Tally hasn't called the past week since she knows that *your* grandmother's coming to town and we're busy getting ready for her."

I loved Killian's mother almost as much as I loved his sister. Serena had welcomed me in, despite the fact that I wasn't a shifter. In fact, a lot of wolf shifters had problems with those of us who were witchblood, but Serena and William O'Connell had taken me in as one of theirs the moment they heard we were engaged.

"We'll invite them both over to meet Nonny. I love your mother. In fact, she spoils the mean mother-in-law cliché." I turned. "How do I look? Properly attired for a funeral?"

I chose a black wrap dress with the silver belt for the funeral. As a nod to the weather, I was wearing knee-high boots, but I made sure they were a sedate black leather with minimal hardware.

Killian was buttoning the jacket for his black suit. "You

look beautifully understated." He glanced at the clock. "I guess we should go."

As we headed down the stairs, I hoped the funeral wouldn't take too long. I had a list a mile long of things I still had to do before Nonny arrived.

CHAPTER TWO

As we approached the funeral home, I found my mood spiraling. I couldn't pinpoint why I was depressed. There was really no reason—even though we were going to a funeral, I hadn't known the deceased. And while Killian was sad, he wasn't distraught. Actually, when I thought about it, I wasn't sure if what I was feeling was even depression.

I felt vaguely uneasy, as though I were waiting for a massive storm to break. Every nerve in my body felt aware and hypervigilant, so much so that it felt like a headache was on the horizon.

We parked in the side lot, and then, as I took Killian's arm, we made our way into the funeral home. After signing the guest book, we followed one of the attendants into a small room. There were five rows of five chairs each, though only about half of them were filled. The casket sat at the front of the room, with a spray of white lilies and ferns covering the bottom half. The top was open, and I silently groaned. The last thing I wanted to do was look at a corpse.

For me, the spirit world was already too near. I preferred not to see the body as well.

Killian led me to the third row and we took the outer two chairs. A middle-aged couple sat in the front left row, along with two men and a woman who looked about Killian's age. I assumed that was the family. The front right row held two elderly couples, and my guess was that they were the grandparents. The second row on the right side was filled with men around Killian's age, and there were three more men on the left side. As we took our seats, several of them turned around and gave Killian a wave.

I leaned toward him and whispered, "Are those your buddies from your camping days?"

"Yes, several of them. I don't know who the three on the left are. I assume they're Darby's friends from somewhere else."

I didn't see any women there except for family members and for me. "Aren't any of your friends married?" I asked, keeping my voice low.

Killian shook his head, giving me a quick look. "Most of them aren't the type to settle down. That's one reason why I stopped hanging out with them. I wanted stability and a relationship. They wanted to just keep hanging out at the bars on Friday nights, hitting on women."

I straightened, watching as the officiant took his place at the podium in front. He tapped the microphone awkwardly, then motioned to the attendant at the back. The attendant closed the door as the organist began to play a dirge, which sent my precarious mood plummeting even further. I had meant it when I told Killian I wanted to support him, but there was part of me that wished I had begged off.

As the officiant began to speak, introducing himself as Darby's best friend, it was obvious that he was trying to find good things to say about the man. At least, good things that the family wouldn't object to.

My attention wandering, I glanced around the room. Darby's family was in obvious mourning, but all of his friends just looked uncomfortable. I had the feeling they were the type of friends who would be there when you had booze, but if you were poor and needed a place to crash, they'd suddenly have things to do. How Killian had gotten mixed up with the group eluded me. Surely, he had never been like them?

I scanned the area for any sign of Darby. There were spirits walking the halls of the funeral home. Not only was the Veil thin due to the approaching holy day, but most funeral homes and mortuaries had spirits attached to them. They were usually the newly dead who hadn't gotten their bearings yet.

It was then that I noticed a little girl in the corner. She was watching the proceedings, but she had that stretched, transparent look of spirits who had been dead for some time. She caught my eye, but instead of looking startled that I could see her, she merely waved and smiled. I was curious why she was here, but given we were in the middle of the service, I wasn't going to disrupt matters by approaching her to strike up a conversation.

I was drifting further into my thoughts when Killian nudged me. Startled, I looked up to see that people were starting to form a line to view the body. Relieved that the evening was almost over, I followed him into the queue. As I linked my arm with his, one of the men in front of us turned around, giving me the once-over. He held my gaze for an uncomfortably long moment before turning back to Killian.

"It's been a while. It's good to see you again." He sounded vaguely bored.

"Yes, it has been a while. Let me introduce my fiancée. January, this is Ken. Ken Jacoby, may I present January

Jaxson? Soon to be my *wife*." Killian emphasized the word, giving Ken a look that seemed to hold a veiled warning.

Ken held out his hand and I reluctantly took it. His fingers were cool, as chilly as his gaze.

"It's nice to meet you, although the circumstances aren't ideal. So, you've captured Killian's heart, have you? I didn't think anybody would ever manage that. You must have some special power. We're going out for a drink afterward. Would you like to join us? It'll be like old times, only without Darby there to make a drunken mess of it."

The callousness with which he spoke startled me.

Killian shook his head. "January and I would love to join you, but we have plans for the evening. Thank you for the invitation." There was a certain brusqueness in his voice that only came out when he was being protective of me. Though I wasn't sure what nuances were taking place beneath the surface, I gratefully placed my other hand on his arm.

Ken didn't want to take no for an answer. "Oh, come, now. We haven't seen each other in years. Don't you want to get together with the old gang? Raise a glass to Darby's memory?" He motioned to me. "And you can introduce January to the others."

Even though I had developed an immediate, visceral dislike of Ken, I didn't want Killian to miss out on seeing his friends. "If you want to go, you can." I paused. I didn't want to make Killian sound like he was lying, so I added, "I have to…finish the cooking for tomorrow, but I can do it alone if you really want to go."

"If it's easier, we can come over to your house," Ken interjected.

Killian shot him a dark look, but merely said, "That's up to January. We're preparing for company." He turned to me. "Are you sure it won't be a bother?"

I could tell that he didn't want to invite Ken—or any of

the others—over, but it felt like the right thing to do. However, I *could* put some limitations on the visit.

"We have about an hour once we get home. But if you're good with that time frame, then yes, you're welcome to come to my house."

Killian sounded anything but happy when he said, "If you think we can spare an hour, then I'll text you the directions. But January really is on a tight schedule so we'll have to close things down by eight." He glanced at me. "In fact, is Darby here?"

Ken looked confused. "What? Darby's dead, man."

"My fiancée is a talented member of the witchblood, and she can sense spirits." Killian smiled slyly as Ken pulled back.

I cleared my throat. *Of course*. If they were all wolf shifters, chances were that at least a few of them would be shy around magic. I made a show of looking around, though I already knew the answer. "If he is, he's keeping quiet. However, there *is* a little girl over in the corner watching the funeral. She waved at me earlier. I have no idea who she is. She's around six or seven, wearing a pink dress, and she seems quite comfortable."

Ken swallowed. "That's his sister. She's probably waiting for him. Darby lost his little sister when she was seven. Vishy drowned in a lake and though Darby tried to save her, he couldn't. I don't think he ever forgave himself for that." For a moment, he seemed vulnerable, and I liked him a little better. "Are you sure about tonight? If you're really too busy, I understand. It's just been a long time and we miss this dude here."

Killian relented. "All right. Here's January's address. But only till eight—we have a lot of chores to finish up tonight. We'll see you there after the funeral's over. But nobody's getting drunk, understand?"

Ken nodded. "Yeah, I hear you." He glanced at the text Killian had sent him. "We'll see you there. I guess I have to get this over with. I've never been good around death." He turned face front and headed toward the casket.

Killian leaned in near my ear. "I'm sorry about this in advance."

"He doesn't seem such a bad sort," I whispered back.

And truth was, he didn't. Now that I'd had a chance to examine Ken's energy, I was beginning to see beneath the cool exterior. I sensed a vulnerable man there, someone who covered up his feelings to protect his heart, and it made me wonder what had hurt him to erect those barriers.

When it was our turn to approach the casket, I began to get cold chills down my back. Something felt off, and I wasn't sure what it was. All day, I'd felt like there was something askew in my world, but I hadn't been able to pinpoint what. At first I'd chalked it up to Killian's call about Darby, and now I thought I'd probably been right.

I glanced around again, looking to see if Darby had made an appearance yet, but his spirit was nowhere to be seen. However, *something* seemed to be hanging around on the astral other than the little girl. In fact, whatever it was, I thought it might be watching me.

The casket was a hideous monstrosity, looking strong enough to withstand a nuclear bomb. Those of us who were witchblood tended to prefer cremation and green burial. We didn't believe in taking up space on the planet with gaudy shows of immortality, especially since we were most likely just coming around again on the Wheel when it was time. Oh, the pyramids and mausoleums like the Taj Mahal were beautiful, but caskets buried in the ground, meant to withstand decay, seemed to thumb their noses at Mother Earth, and they resisted the cycle of birth and death.

Inside the casket lay Darby, still and silent. His eyes were closed, and a coin rested on his forehead. I assumed it was a family tradition. He was a slight man, and even in death there was an unpleasant sneer on his face. I couldn't explain it, but I felt like somehow I knew him.

I'd never met the man, but I knew men like him and, even without Killian's input, one look at this corpse would have told me what kind of man Darby had been in life. He was wiry and thin, and looked older than Killian, but I suspected that was probably from drug or alcohol abuse. He had beautiful long red hair, and I wondered what color his eyes been.

Blue.

I jumped as the word slammed into my head. Looking around, I once again scanned the room for Darby's spirit, but he was nowhere in sight. The little girl was still in the corner, but when I glanced at her, she just stared at her parents. It was obvious she missed them, and I wished I could go up and tell them she was here, but this wasn't the time or place. They had just lost their second child, and they had to be devastated.

The reception droned on, but we only stayed for a few minutes. Killian spoke to Darby's parents, but I hung back. They didn't need to meet me in their grief. Then, after a brief word with Ken, Killian took my elbow and steered me out into the storm that had broken while we were in the funeral home. A huge flash of lightning split the sky as we left the building, followed by a rumble that shook the ground.

"The storm's right over us. Let's get home," I said, trying to fend off the rain that slashed sideways. In western Washington, sideways rain was a very real thing, egged on by the winds that came slicing through the area. Even as I spoke, a gust sprang up, blasting through as it chilled me to the bone.

"Hurry," Killian shouted, and we made a run for the car. He bundled me into the passenger side, then hurried to slide into the driver's seat. "If this is any indication of what the rest of autumn and winter is going to be like, we'd better get ready for power outages."

As we sat in the car, waiting for the heater to warm up, I nodded. "I want to look into hardwiring a generator into the house." Pausing, I added, "Whichever house we decide on, that is." We were still debating whether to live in my house—which was too small—or Killian's house, which wasn't my house.

As Killian pulled out of the parking lot, he breathed a sigh of relief. "I owe you one. That has to be one of the worst evenings we've spent. It was excruciating. I'm sorry it's not over yet, but I won't let them stay long. Ken was always the leader of the group, and Darby was the outlier. He never really fit in, but we let him hang around because he didn't have any other friends. But watch out for Ken—he's a womanizer. I don't trust him around gorgeous women, taken or not."

"Hon," I said, "I'm not putting myself down—really—but I doubt that I'm his type. He seems to be the kind of man looking for a woman who's more like a Victoria's Secret model."

"You'd be surprised," Killian muttered. "Ken dated women of all sizes and colors when we hung out together." He paused, then asked, "So you didn't see Darby?"

"No, but I'm pretty sure I felt him around. I wish I could have told his parents about the little girl, but it didn't seem the right time."

"I think you were right in keeping that quiet. For one thing, they're skittish of magic and even more skittish around ghosts. I don't think your news would have had the desired effect. I mainly feel sorry that you couldn't help her move on."

I shook my head. "I don't think she's trapped. I think she chose to be there. Maybe she subconsciously comforted them or something."

"Well, either way, thank you for going with me. I appreciate it. I'm just sorry it was so grim." He swung onto the street leading to our homes.

"I don't know about that." I laughed. "I've had a lot of harrowing evenings on the job. This wasn't the worst of them, by far."

"*Not* the same thing. Come on, I'll pull together refreshments. You don't have to lift a finger." He waited for me, then we made a dash for the porch.

As we entered the house and turned on the lights, the cats yawned from where they were curled on the sofa. I took one look at them and decided to tuck them away in our bedroom.

"I think I'm going to take them upstairs. I don't want anybody accidentally letting them out," I said. Truth was, I didn't trust Ken and his buddies to be careful with the door.

Killian twisted his lip. "Yeah, probably for the best. I'll get started in the kitchen."

Luring Xi and Klaus up to the spare bedroom with kitty treats, I shed my coat, changed into a comfortable but cute jersey dress, and touched up my makeup. As I was headed down to the kitchen, the doorbell rang and I hurried to answer it.

I opened the door to find the four men standing there, with Ken in front. I let them in, ushering them into the living room. "Won't you come in? Killian will be with you shortly."

Ken set a bottle on the coffee table. It was some sort of whisky—an expensive brand by the looks of it. He waved the other three toward the sofa and they gingerly sat down.

"Thank you for inviting us," Ken said. He introduced the others. "This is Jaimie, Hershel—we call him Hersh—and Richie." He glanced at the men. "This is January. Killian's woman—*fiancée*."

I didn't bristle. I knew that among wolf shifters, calling your mate your "woman" was par for the course. Killian seldom slipped but every now and then he introduced me as such.

"Welcome to my home. I'm so sorry about your friend." I wanted to slip into the kitchen to help Killian but I had better manners than that. "Please, sit down."

I was about to offer to get them some glasses for their booze when Killian entered the living room, carrying a large tray on which sat a platter of sandwiches and a bowl of chips. He set the tray on the coffee table and noticed the whisky.

"I'll get glasses. January, you want one?"

I shook my head. "Not with Nonny getting in tomorrow. And I don't get along well with whisky anyway. I'll take a glass of wine, though, if you would."

"Your wish is my command, my love," he said, vanishing back into the kitchen.

"How long have you and Killian been together?" Hersh asked. He was a harsh-looking man, but his voice was surprisingly gentle.

"Two years. I moved back to Moonshadow Bay about six months after my parents died in a car crash. This was their house. I was just getting out of a really bad marriage, so I decided I might as well stay. My best friend lives here, too, and that factored into matters. Killian was moving in right about the same time as I was. He lives next door." I couldn't help but smile as I thought about our meeting.

For a moment they said nothing. Then Ken said, "I'm sorry about your parents."

"It's all right," I said, thinking back to the day I'd gotten the call from the police. I tried to brush it out of my mind, though, and cleared my throat. "Are all of you from California?"

As one they nodded. Then Ken said, "I was born up here, like Darby. That's how we met. We decided to take a chance on California together and once we were down there, we met Hersh, Killian, and Richie. We were all hanging out at the same sports bar after work and just bonded." He paused, then said, "Killian looks good. You're good for him."

Surprised, I smiled. "Thank you. We're good for each other."

"I think somehow you're the one who's the better influence. So, what do you do?" Ken motioned for Hersh, who was about to say something, to stay quiet.

Feeling a little awkward, I said, "I work for Conjure Ink, a paranormal investigations organization. We check out urban legends, go ghost hunting—that's primarily my forte—and take on all sorts of monster reports. We actually had a Mothman visitation this year, and went after Bigfoot. Neither one ended well."

Killian appeared, another tray in hand with glasses and my wine. He set it down next to the sandwiches. "What did I miss?"

"Your fiancée is bad-ass, man. I'd be scared out of my skin to do what she does." Ken sounded sincere, again surprising me. He poured whisky in the glasses, then held his drink in the air. "Here's to January. Killian doesn't deserve you!" He laughed as he said it, but his words set me on edge.

But before I could say anything, Killian chimed in. "I know that. I really don't. But as long as she's willing to put up with me, I'm happy."

I leaned toward him, shaking my head. "You're not the *only* lucky one. I wouldn't marry someone I didn't respect and you know it. I'll never compromise myself again."

"I'll never treat you the way Ellison did," Killian said.

Again, feeling like I was quickly becoming the focus, I lifted my goblet of wine. "I'd like to propose a toast to your friend Darby. May he find his rest, and I hope his sister was able to help him." I told the others about Darby's little sister.

"Darby's folks have been hit pretty bad. All three of their kids are dead now," Richie said.

"Three?" Killian asked. "I never knew about a third sibling. Darby talked about his little sister, but…"

"Oh yeah," Hersh said. "Darby had an older brother. Rusty. Darby had substance issues, but Rusty—he really slid down the spiral. He got himself hooked on steroids. He was a gym bunny. He wanted to compete and he would do anything to win. He went all 'roid rage one day while driving. Tried to sideswipe a car that cut him off and went into a tailspin. His truck spun off one of the overpasses and crashed on the freeway below."

"Holy crap. I'm guessing he didn't make it out?" The fact that one family had three such tragic losses threw me. Once was bad, twice might be coincidence, but three children—all tragically struck down? That pushed beyond the "Oh gee, how horrible" stage into the question of "What's behind all this?"

"He was trapped inside. The driver's door jammed when he went off the overpass. When they retrieved his remains, they ascertained that his back was broken during the fall. The truck went up in flames with Rusty unable to get out. Even if he had been able to open the door, his injuries would have prevented him from escaping."

"And no one was around to help?"

"No, this was back in the 1970s before cell phones. And the drivers nearby were afraid to approach the truck because gas was pouring out of it. Rusty was trying to make it in bodybuilding. Back then, steroid use was common, and he wanted to be among the best. He idolized Franco Columbo and Arnold Schwarzenegger and Lou Ferrigno. Of course, Rusty couldn't compete in the regular contests due to the fact that he was a wolf shifter—but he aspired to the Otherkin versions." Ken shrugged.

"What did Darby think of this?"

"He idolized his brother. He wasn't interested in bodybuilding, but he grew up thinking Rusty could do no wrong. Their parents were blind to *all* of the problems their children had. After Rusty died, they shut down." Ken shrugged. "Darby did everything he could to make them happy, but when his little sister Vishy drowned and he wasn't able to save her, they blamed him. It wasn't his fault—the water was so cold that Darby almost drowned trying to reach her. He had to turn around and come back."

"Where were their parents?" Killian asked. "I never knew about this."

"They had let Darby and his sister go to the lake by themselves while they were visiting Rusty's grave in a nearby cemetery." Ken shook his head. "Darby's parents blamed him. He had moved out of the house by then, but he still dropped by to hang out with his sister. He adored her and Vishy clung to him for attention since their parents were still fixated on Rusty. After she died, Darby and I decided to head to California. There wasn't anything tying him to the area, and I was ready for a change."

I glanced at Killian. Sometimes, people had backstories that made me want to cry. I thought about Vishy and wondered if she was still mourning the attention she never received. Maybe she had come to meet Darby because he had been the only one who cared about her.

"Man, this is not the wake I expected," Richie said. "But then again, we're talking about Darby." He said it with such a snarky tone that I wanted to smack him. His words were also slurred, leading me to think he was already drunk.

Apparently Killian felt the same way, because he cleared his throat. "I thought honoring someone's memory was the point, and that's what we've been doing." He pointed at the whisky bottle, which was three-quarters empty. "You've singlehandedly emptied most of that, and I don't want you driving on the road. Did you come with someone else?"

"He rode with me," Hersh said. "And I've only had one drink. I think we should head back to the hotel. Come on, Rich. Let's get you back to the room."

"Already? Gods, Killian, you've changed. You never would have shut down the party this earlier a few years ago. *Pussy-whipped* is an understatement—"

But Richie didn't get a chance to finish the statement. Killian was on his feet, hustling him to the door before anybody else had a chance to speak.

"You will *not* use that phrase around my fiancée, or around me. I grew up and I learned how to control my mouth. I also learned how to respect women. *You* could take a lesson from me."

Hersh rushed over to take Richie off Killian's hands. "I'll get him out to the car. Sorry, man. Darby wasn't the only one who didn't know when to keep his mouth shut, but Richie has far fewer reasons. He's been hitting the sauce pretty hard."

"I'm so sorry," Ken said to me. "I really didn't want any scenes like this. Please don't think I'm like Richie. I'm not."

Something about his apology struck me as odd, but I decided to ignore it. I just wanted them all to go home. I was depressed about Darby's life and his sister, Ken was giving me odd vibes, and I was ready to shut the door on them.

Killian saw them out while I carried the trays back into the kitchen. They had taken the rest of the whisky with them, or I would have poured it out. The spaghetti sauce was ready, so I ladled it into a low, flat container so that it would cool quickly when I refrigerated it.

Killian peeked in while I was sorting out the dishes. He apologetically grimaced at me. "I'm sorry about them."

"You warned me. But hey, you paid your respects to Darby. It sounds like he had a rough life. I'm glad that's over."

"I dunno... I won't feel easy for a few days. Death goes in threes, you know." Killian said it with such a deadpan face that I wasn't sure if he was being flippant.

"What?"

"My mother used to say that. Death goes in threes. Over the years, I've seen that happen more often than is comfortable. But whatever the case, tonight's over. Tomorrow we can go back to focusing on our own lives. Do we have plans in the morning?"

"Teran's coming over in the morning to help us finish getting ready. Rowan and I talked about getting together in the afternoon, since Nonny doesn't get in till later, so we might as well go. Rowan and I want to discuss our plans for dealing with Gretchen. And Tarvish bought a new pool table he wants to show you. Ari's coming over Sunday night for a movie night."

I paused, then looked up at Killian. "Your friends seem so different than you."

"They are, now." Killian's eyes flared. "There was a time we all fit together, but I've left all that behind and I don't regret it." He took the dishcloth out of my hand. "Come upstairs. Love me. Let me fuck you."

And just like that, the mood shifted, and I followed him to the bedroom.

"I want you so bad," he said, leading me up the stairs.

A shiver ran through me, from the tip of my head to the bottom of my feet, but the feeling settled between my thighs. I caught my breath. Killian was an attentive lover. We had begun exploring our kinky sides, and I was surprised that we meshed so well in that manner. I had never realized that I really wasn't vanilla. Sex with Ellison had been boring for both of us. But my sex play with Killian had brought out my more flavorful side, and we routinely brought blindfolds and velvet ropes and paddle boards into the bedroom. I had discovered that I *did* have a submissive side, but only between the sheets, and only if I trusted the person I was with.

"Take the lead. I will follow."

And so Killian led me up the stairs, away from thoughts of old friends long gone, and away from the stillness of death, toward a validation of life itself.

CHAPTER THREE

"Strip for me." The light in Killian's eyes told me he was in his alpha mood. I hadn't realized how much of an alpha wolf he was. Luckily, he wasn't obnoxious about it, and in the bedroom, I enjoyed his dominance.

I kicked off my shoes and unbuckled my belt. Xi and Klaus were still in the guest room, but they had food and water and a litter box and they'd be all right. I turned as Killian led me into the bedroom, his eyes smoldering. He sat down in the oversized armchair in the corner, his gaze fastened on me.

"Take off your clothes," he said, his voice husky.

I faced him, tossing the belt over the quilt rack to my left. Then, I slowly lifted my dress, pulling the jersey over my head. I draped it over the quilt rack as well, and turned back to him. I was wearing my matching cobalt blue lace bra and panties set. The lace was actually microfiber, so it was pretty while still comfortable. The underwire was strong enough to bear up the weight of my boobs. I never felt awkward around Killian, even though I was a large woman. He loved my curves, and I never felt lacking.

"What next?" I asked, challenging him to take control.

He met my dare. "Take off your panties."

I shimmied out of my panties and tossed them in the laundry basket, then turned back to him.

"Now take off your bra. I want to see your breasts bounce free."

I unhooked my bra and draped it over the quilt rack, standing naked in front of him.

"What should I do next?" I could barely breathe, I was so horny. I wanted him, wanted him to thrust his thick, hard cock inside of me. I wanted to feel his lips on my breasts, his fingers between my legs. I wanted him to touch me.

"Fondle yourself with your right hand, and squeeze your breasts and nipples with your left. Pleasure yourself for me. You look so wanton when you're horny."

He stood, stripping off his shirt and pants and tossing them to the side. His muscles gleamed under the light, and his cock stood rigid, fully at attention, springing thickly out of the hair surrounding the trunk. He was throbbing, turgid with desire.

I parted my thighs and gently slid my hand between them, stroking myself. With my other hand, I reached up and began to circle my nipple, pinching until it was hard. Killian focused on me, and his attention turned me on even more. The warmth in my belly turned to heat, and I began to circle my clit harder, my breath quickening. I wanted him, I wanted him to throw me onto the bed, to take me and prove that I was his, to thrust his shaft into my core. Killian was well endowed, not so much that it hurt, but enough so that I *knew* when he was inside me.

"That's it, keep going baby," he said, his eyes gleaming with a feral light. His wolf was rising to the surface, and I was grateful he knew how to rein it in so that he wouldn't shift and disrupt our sex play. "Harder. Rub yourself harder."

I sped up the motion, grinding against my hand. I knew what he wanted, and I began to inch toward the bed.

"What do you want next? Tell me what to do." It was a challenge, a dare to see how far he would push me. I trusted him never to force me into something I couldn't handle, and so far he had never crossed the line.

He licked his lips, crossing toward me. He pointed toward the bed. "Down. I want to watch you fuck yourself."

I slid across the bed, my breasts bouncing with their heavy weight. Opening the nightstand drawer, I brought out a large dildo, holding it up for his approval.

"Should I use this one?"

His breath still ragged, he nodded. "Lube it up. I want you to fuck yourself so hard you scream. Use the vibrator, too. Show me what you like." He was gripping his cock, his fist tightly wrapped around it.

I brought out the bullet vibrator as well, then leaned up against the headboard. Bending my knees, I spread my legs and pressed the vibrator against my clit, turning it on high. Then, I slowly eased the dildo toward my vaj, running it around my slit. The vibrator was doing its work, and my breath began to quicken as my nipples stood at attention.

"Fuck yourself, baby. Take it all in. Up to the hilt." By now, Killian was sitting at the edge of the bed staring intently between my legs. He squeezed his cock, and drops of pre-cum appeared at the tip, glistening in the dim light.

Trembling, I positioned the dildo and, with a powerful stroke, thrust it inside me, moaning as the girthy toy filled me up. The vibrator continued to dance against my clit, and the sensation of Killian watching me as I masturbated only heightened my arousal. I began to moan, unable to keep silent. I bucked, gyrating my hips. Killian let out a low growl, his fist squeezing his cock so hard that it was turning red.

The next moment, he let go and rolled the condom down the length of his shaft.

With one hand he grabbed the dildo away from me. I moved the vibrator as he lowered his head between my legs and began to bathe me with his tongue, pressing hard against my nub as he held onto my hips with his hands, pulling me tight against his face.

I tried to shift, to thrust against him, but he held me fast. Reaching up, I began to rub my breasts, squeezing my nipples hard until they hurt. The pain only heightened the sensation and I reached down, clenching the covers as I attempted to catch my breath. But I couldn't, he was driving me wild, and my pulse thundered in my head.

Then, before I could come, he rose up and plunged inside me, penetrating to my deepest core. As he pounded against me, I raised my legs up and wrapped them around his waist. He dipped his head and dragged his teeth across one of my nipples, tweaking lightly. Stretched wide by his girth, swollen with desire, I slid my hand between us, continuing to stroke myself as he thrust into me. I gasped for breath, unable to resist the siren song any longer. I let go and caved, wave after wave of orgasm rippling through me. And then Killian joined me, our cries mingling together as we came hard and fast until the only sounds left in the room were our exhausted breathing as he collapsed against me, spent.

After a moment, he rolled over and carefully removed the condom, using a tissue from the nightstand to wipe off his penis.

I faced him, curling on my side. "Well. Just...*well*."

Killian reached out and stroked my cheek. He smiled, his cheeks crinkling. "You are *all* woman, January. You drive me crazy in the best of all possible ways." He paused, then asked, "Was it good for you? Do you need anything else?"

I laughed. "It was *so* good. And no, I'm satisfied—" I

paused, suddenly becoming aware that there was something off. In the midst of our sex play I hadn't noticed it, but now I felt like there was something was hanging over my shoulder. Anxious, I pushed myself up against the headboard and looked around.

"Is anything wrong?" Killian asked.

I worried my lip for a moment, but I couldn't put my finger on anything in particular. Chalking it up to a stressful day, I shook my head. "No, everything's okay. I'm probably just tired. Why don't we take a shower and go to sleep early? We need to finish cleaning before Nonny gets here, and I don't want to wait until the last minute."

Obligingly, he took my hand and led me into the bathroom. We shared the walk-in shower, lathering each other up. He pulled me against him, leaning down to give me a long kiss. As I leaned my head against his shoulder, once again I gave thanks that we had found each other. I loved Killian more than I had ever thought possible.

But in the back of my mind, I still felt uneasy. It was probably just the nervousness over Nonny's impending visit, as well as attending a funeral. I pushed it out of my thoughts as we toweled off and dried our hair and then went to bed.

All night long, though, I dreamed of a strange mist that obscured everything. And even in my dreams, I felt like something was obscuring my sight.

Teran arrived at ten. She came around back, tapping on the kitchen door before entering.

The storm hadn't knocked out power, though we were still due for high winds over the next few days. There were branches down and tipped-over trash bins, so Killian was outside, picking up the debris while I read the news and finished my latte and a piece of the sample cake.

"Good morning. Coffee?" My aunt's eyes sparkled. I adored her—she was a free spirit and while I had loved my mother, I had spent a lot of my teen years hanging out with Teran. Now, at seventy-one, she was active, vital, and very open about her opinions. She also changed her color every two months and now, she had a rainbow of autumn colors streaking her hair.

"I thought I'd help you—whatever you need—and then run out and grocery shop. Mother's staying with me for a week, after tonight. You knew that, right?"

I nodded. "I took this week off, but there are a lot of autumn chores to do around here. So that will work out for the best, especially since Nonny's going to be here for two weeks. You want some cake?"

"Ooo, what do you have?" Teran sat down beside me. "Did you decide on a flavor for the wedding cake?"

"We did. Would you like to try the sample?" I cut a slice of the chocolate-raspberry and handed it to her. "This is our choice. And here's a picture of what the cake will look like." I pulled out my phone and showed her the email that Carrie had sent me after we finalized our decision. "Otherwise, though, yesterday was weird." I told her about the unexpected funeral and the aborted wake. "I don't know—it was all just so odd and uncomfortable."

"I imagine. It sounds awkward." She paused, then added, "Speaking of awkward, what are you going to tell my mother about the present she sent you?"

I grimaced. "I don't know, to be honest. She didn't include any letter in the crate and all she would say is that she'd tell me about it when she got here. Do you know anything?"

Nonny had sent me a present. It was an antique rolltop desk. It had just arrived a few days back, and I was still sorting it out. Unfortunately, while it was lovely, it didn't fit my décor, and I had no clue of where to put it.

"I remember it was in our living room when I was little. Mother told me that it belonged to your great-great-grandmother. The one who started this whole mess with the curse. That's all I know."

"Great-great-grandma, huh? Well, another piece of the puzzle. We were talking about going over to Rowan's this afternoon. You want to come with us? Rowan and I are going to discuss how to confront Gretchen about the curse."

"Better sooner than later. None of us is rewinding the clock." Teran finished her cake. "I'll do whatever you need me to, you know. The family curse involves me, too."

"Yeah." I sighed. "I know."

The women in my family were under a curse. We were doomed to die too soon, thanks to a curse placed on us by a powerful witch, long ago in Ireland. My great-great-grandmother had been accused of cursing a local farmer or something, and that farmer hired Gretchen Wyre, another witch, to hex our entire family. She'd done a good job. Too good. Now, thanks to the internet, we knew where she was living—Seattle. It was time to confront the witch and make her break the curse.

I was carrying my mug and plate to the counter when Esmara appeared. She was wearing a dress I'd never seen—it was black, Victorian in style, and Esmara had a somber look on her face. She was one of Nonny's sisters, also gone on too soon thanks to the curse, and now she was part of the Ladies, our family's guardians. Esmara was essentially my spirit guide.

"Esmara! What are you doing here? You look—" I paused as she shook her head.

"Esmara's here?" Teran asked, looking around. "Odd, I don't sense her."

I need to talk to you and it needs to be in private. Esmara crooked her finger, motioning for me to follow her.

"I'll be right back," I said. "I...need to check on something." I followed Esmara out of the kitchen. She led me to my office.

Shut the door so Teran can't hear you talking.

Bewildered, I did as she asked. "What's going on? What happened?"

You need to sit down. I have news and you must be prepared in order to help Teran when it officially arrives. Esmara's tone was both brusque and sad.

I sat down in my office chair. "What's going on, Esmara?"

Either you or Teran will be receiving word within a few hours. Naomi's plane crashed, right into the ocean. I imagine the earliest reports will be on the news if you take a look. I want you to be prepared to help Teran. She and Nonny had a troubled relationship in many ways, and it's going to be hard on her. She'll have conflicting emotions.

My heart stood still for a moment. Nonny was *dead*? How could that be true? I sat there for a moment, emotions waging war within me. I wanted to cry, but I found myself strangely bereft of tears. I wasn't numb—my heart felt heavy —but the shock of the news had left me almost unable to respond.

"I don't understand," I finally said. "How do you know?"

Because Prue was there to walk her through the Veil. It was the curse, January—it finally caught up to Naomi. Esmara rested a ghostly hand on my shoulder and, even though I couldn't feel the weight of her touch, it was still comforting.

"Do you know if anybody survived the crash? Where did the plane go down?" I opened my laptop and quickly brought up a major news site. Sure enough, one of the headlines read
IRISH ISLES FLIGHT REPORTED MISSING OFF GREENLAND

COAST. Sure enough, Nonny had taken one of the Irish Isles flights.

The article was short—simply stating that Flight 1182 from Irish Isles Airlines had vanished off the radar over the Davis Strait between the coast of Greenland and Baffin Island, and that investigators had begun searching for remains.

I pulled up Nonny's email with the details of her trip and checked the flight number. Sure enough—she'd been scheduled for Flight 1182. Pushing my computer back, I turned to Esmara, feeling battered and numb.

"Nonny's really dead, isn't she?"

I'm afraid so. You have to be strong for Teran. There were a lot of strains on the relationship. Naomi was going to try to resolve some of them when she visited. Now, that won't happen. And Teran won't be able to see or talk to Nonny for a while—just like you haven't been able to talk to your mother yet.

I sat there for another minute, trying to figure out how to approach Teran. "Should I tell her or wait for the call?"

If you wait for the call and she finds out you knew already, Teran will be furious. No, you need to prepare her. As far as whether anybody survived, I don't think so, but I can't be sure.

"Did she suffer? Was it quick?" I wanted something—some little tidbit to offer some comfort to Teran.

Yes, it was quick. And no, she didn't suffer. She didn't expect this, but Prue said she wasn't confused or anything. Esmara paused, then added, *I'm sorry, January. I know you loved your grandmother, but Teran's lost her mother, and this is going to be very hard on her. All right, I have to get back. I'm helping Prue with Naomi's transition. But I'll be around if you need me.*

And then, just like that, she vanished.

CHAPTER FOUR

I wasn't sure what to do, so the first thing I did was text Killian, who was out back. I NEED YOU TO COME INSIDE. I HAVE SOME NEWS TO BREAK TO TERAN AND I COULD USE THE SUPPORT.

WHAT HAPPENED? ARE YOU OKAY?

I'M FINE, YES. BUT PLEASE COME INTO THE KITCHEN.

I'LL BE RIGHT THERE, he texted back.

Then I texted Rowan and asked if she could come over. I told her what had happened and she said she'd be right over. Finally, after printing out the brief account from the news site, I steeled myself and headed back to the kitchen.

Teran was immersed in reading a novel. I doubted that she had realized how long I had been gone. I was trying not to cry. It was my turn to be the strong one. My tears could wait for a little while. If Teran really did have as many unresolved issues with her mother as Esmara said she did, then the next few months weren't going to be easy for either of us.

I waited until Killian came in from the backyard. He gave me a questioning look, but I shook my head and asked him if he would fix a pot of tea.

At that, Teran looked up. "Tea? You don't drink tea."

"No, but you do. I've called Rowan and she's on the way over." I hesitated, unsure of how to begin. But Teran gave me an opening.

"Is Esmara still here? What did she want?" Teran placed the bookmark in the fold of her book, then closed it and set it aside.

"I have something to tell you and it's not going to be easy." I hesitated again as Killian crossed to the counter and put the kettle on. He opened several tea bags and put them into my strawberry-covered teapot. Then he brought over a tray with four cups and saucers on it.

"Well, sometimes it's easiest to start at the beginning." Teran gave me a wary look, the vague hint of worry in her eyes. "Something's very wrong, isn't it?"

I nodded. "Yes, something is *very* wrong. I don't know how to tell you this, so I'll just come out and say it. Esmara told me that Nonny's plane crashed in the ocean. She didn't survive." I practically had to rip the words out of my throat to set them free.

Teran stared at me, her bewilderment slowly turning to understanding. It was like watching a building crash. At first, the edges go, and then suddenly the main support explodes and everything tumbles inward in one big implosion.

"My mother's dead?"

I hurried around the table to give her a hug. Wrapping my arms around her shoulders, I held her tight, wanting her to know I was there for her.

"Yes, I'm afraid so. Prue was there to meet her. I gather that Prue and Esmara decided that it would be best if I told you rather than you finding out from the airline, or from Prue herself. The plane went down in the Davis Strait, off the coast of Greenland. Or at least it vanished from radar. But Nonny told Esmara that it crashed." I set down the paper I had printed off the news site. "This is the only official word about it yet, but I imagine that the airline will be contacting us pretty soon. I'm so sorry, Teran. Esmara said it was the curse."

Teran sat there, staring at the center of the table. Killian's jaw dropped, but he said nothing as he brought the teapot over to place it next to the cups. Without being prompted, he poured three cups of tea and sat one of them in front of Teran. He carried one to the other end of the table, and I picked up the third. The fourth would be for Rowan when she got here.

"May the gods damn Val Slater's grandfather to hell, and may he rot there."

The grandfather of Val Slater, the local godfather of vampires, had paid Gretchen Wyre to curse the family. It all led back to his feud with Ellen ó Broin.

Teran stared into her tea for a moment, then suddenly burst into tears. I didn't see my aunt cry that often, but today made up for it. Her shoulders heaving, she pushed her teacup back and rested her head on her arms, weeping. I placed my right hand on her left shoulder blade, focusing as much healing energy into her as I could. I knew it was barely a Band-Aid, but there was nothing else I could do. I looked over at Killian, feeling helpless. I wanted to cry, too—the reality was setting in for me now—but Teran needed my strength.

Killian stood and motioned that he would be back in a moment, then hurried out of the room. A few minutes later he came back, his laptop in hand. He set it on the table near his chair, then went to the refrigerator and pulled out a loaf of bread. I watched as he made a stack of toast, heavily buttered, and brought it over.

"My mother always says toast and tea helps the stomach during an upset."

I realize that was his way of trying to help. Silently, I took a slice of toast and sat back down. I really didn't like tea, but the toast was good and Killian was right—it seemed to help settle my stomach a bit.

After a while, Teran raised her head. She looked bewildered, like someone who had stumbled into a nightmare and didn't know how to get out. "I can't believe it. After all this time, the first time in years she decides to visit, and this happens."

"I feel kind of responsible—" I started to say.

"Don't even go there. I know why you're saying that. You weren't the one who decided she would come over now. You weren't the one who decided to wait until now to make the visit. We have no idea whether Gretchen's curse would have hit her ten years ago if she had come over then, or ten years from now." Teran shook her head, and for the first time since I'd known her she looked her age. Grief had a way of making people look old, if only through the immediate shock.

"Is there any more news?" I asked, glancing at Killian.

He was poring through site after site, looking for news of the crash. After a moment, he paused and looked up. "I found a post on Ribbet. It was posted by Hacker-AZ. You know, the group that watchdogs over the government agencies and reports on coverups? They're stating that the United Freedom Liberation Front is claiming responsibility for bringing down the plane."

I caught my breath. The UFLF was an international terrorist group that worked jointly in the UK, Ireland, and the United States. I wasn't sure of its long-term goals, but they claimed to be responsible for a number of bombings.

"I assume that isn't official?" I said.

He shook his head. "No, it's not official. But I can believe it because several important dignitaries from Ireland were on board the flight. And I believe that UFLF has a beef with some of them."

"What are the odds that Nonny would get on board that plane?" I pushed away my teacup. "Would you mind making me a triple-shot latte? I think I need the caffeine."

Teran was trying to dry her eyes and I reached for a box of tissues, handing it to her. She took one and began wiping away the tears. She looked exhausted.

"If Esmara was right and it's the curse that took my mother, then it's not so against the odds. Curses work in ways you'd never think—causing someone to step out at the wrong time into traffic, causing a driver to take a curve at an elevated speed, not realizing there's ice around the corner. The curse could easily have pushed my mother to select this flight."

I bit into another piece of toast. "Why didn't we go down to talk to Gretchen last week?"

Teran didn't even notice what I said. "We *have* to break this. We *have* to get Gretchen to relent, or we have to find a way to break it ourselves. I don't want my life to end at the hands of terrorists or sliding on ice or making a wrong move that I could have easily avoided. And I don't want that for you." She reached across the table and took my hands, holding them tight. Her fingers were cold, and I realized that she was shivering.

As Killian delivered my latte to the table I asked him to please turn up the thermostat a couple degrees. He went to do so just as the doorbell rang.

"I'll get it," he said.

"It's probably Rowan." I glanced over at Teran. "I hope you don't mind, but I asked her to come over."

"I don't mind. Why didn't Prue tell me about this?" Teran looked like she'd been sideswiped.

I was wondering that myself, but I tried to think from the

Ladies' point of view. "I think both she and Esmara thought it would be best coming from me. And Prue was off helping Nonny make the transition. I hate to think that this was a planned attack."

"Oh, if it's UFLF, then you can be sure that the plan was to kill everyone on board. They don't mess around."

Killian returned, Rowan behind him. She immediately crossed to Teran to comfort her.

I needed a break, so I retreated to the back porch. It was a blustery, chilly day, and while it wasn't raining, the air hung heavy with moisture. I crossed my arms, shivering. I could see my breath. I stared out over the backyard, feeling lost. Everything had been turned upside down and I wasn't sure what to do. I had been going to take the week off from work, but I decided to go back in on Monday. If I just sat around, I'd fret. When dealing with a crisis, I worked through it easier if I kept myself busy.

"So, how are you?" Killian asked, joining me. He wrapped his arms around my waist.

"I don't really know," I said. "I need to be strong for my aunt. I'm sad and I keep thinking I should be crying, but the tears aren't there. I loved Nonny, but...I'm beginning to realize how little I knew about her. And then I feel guilty for not being more upset than I am."

"Grief is complicated enough when it's someone really close to you. But it can be a twisted ball of yarn when there are other factors involved. I know you loved her, but love doesn't always mean that you felt really close to her. Feel the way you feel. Don't set expectations on your shoulders that aren't right for you." He turned me around and pulled me to his chest.

I rested my head on his shoulder. "I think I'm afraid Teran will see me as a bad person if I don't break down.

Nonny was her *mother*. Teran went to pieces when *my* mother died, but she was also there for me."

"Althea was Teran's sister. They saw each other *every day*. Of course Teran was a wreck. How often have you seen Nonny?"

I sniffled. "Not since I was little."

"And how often did you two talk?"

I sighed. "A few times on the phone. And we emailed once every month or so. But she was my grandma."

"Yes, but she wasn't a regular fixture in your life. Your parents—of course you fell apart when they died. You loved them, you didn't see them a lot but you talked to your mother all the time on the phone, right?" He tilted my chin up so that I was looking him in the face.

I nodded, swallowing. "Yeah. I guess I'm reacting normally, right? I'm so afraid that I'm being callous that *that* thought's hurting me more than Nonny's actual death, if I'm being honest with myself."

"There is no 'normal' when it comes to how you react to a loss. Really, love. You're not being a horrible person, you're not being callous. You loved Nonny, but you didn't really know her that well and she was barely in your life. Tell me, how do you think you'd feel if Rowan died?"

I shuddered, not wanting to even think about it. "I'd be devastated."

"Yes, because for two years now, she's been a constant in your life. Proximity and connection play into these matters. So, you grieve however you need to grieve. Teran will understand." He gently held me by the shoulders, then swept a lock of hair out of my eyes.

"Thank you, for being you. Thank you for understanding who I am," I said, letting out a long sigh. "Is it any wonder why I love you?"

"Hey, I'm just being honest, and trying to help you face

the reality of your feelings. Don't feel guilty—you have nothing to feel guilty about."

At that moment, the kitchen door opened and Rowan peeked out. "Everything okay with you? How are you faring?"

I sighed. "I'm all right. Sad, feeling in shock but..."

"The airline just called Teran with the news. I took the call for her. It's bad. Nobody survived. Over one hundred passengers and they're *all* dead. The United Freedom Liberation Front has publicly claimed responsibility for the explosion, though it's not verified yet that they're telling the truth. The authorities on both sides of the pond will be investigating. Meanwhile, I'm going to take Teran home with me. I have a tangle of plants that need some TLC and right now, that might do her some good. I wanted to see how you were doing before we leave, though." She looped her arm with mine and we walked over to the screen door leading down to the backyard.

As we surveyed the Mystic Wood that buttressed up against my yard, Rowan kissed my cheek. "I'm sorry about Naomi."

"So am I. I wish I could have known her better." I turned to her and said, "Please, I want to spend more time together. You're the only grandmother I have now. The Jaxsons moved to Scotland, and they barely ever write."

Rowan had entrusted my father, Trevor, to the Jaxsons when he was an infant to keep him safe. I wasn't sure if he'd ever realized that Rowan was his actual mother.

"I promise we'll do more together. Maybe we can start a weekly or bi-weekly dinner?" Rowan wasn't touchy-feely but she did love me. That much I knew.

"As long as we're not reenacting *the Gilmore Girls*' Friday night dinners. Those were horrific." I was crying a little now —mostly because of the stress of the day, though my head was hurting pretty badly from the stress.

"I never watched that show," Rowan said, "but I get it. No, nothing like a Friday night screaming match. All right, since you're in capable hands, I'm going to take Teran home. I'll call or text you later."

Before I could say good-bye, she darted back inside. I shivered again and turned to face the gloom-filled day. At that moment, my phone rang and I glanced at it. Irish Isles Airlines. Sighing, not wanting to talk to them right then, I handed the phone to Killian and turned to go back inside, wondering what to do next.

CHAPTER FIVE

By Sunday, Teran called me to say she was better, though I knew she wasn't. But she had overcome the shock, though we were both avoiding the news because photos of the plane crash were splashed across all the news outlets. A few of the local news stations from around Puget Sound had tried to contact us, but we both just told them "No comment" and left it at that.

Teran insisted she could handle making the arrangements for Nonny's death. There wasn't much left of anybody, which was a gruesome thought, given that the explosion had taken place in midair and the bomb had been in the cargo bay right beneath where Nonny was sitting.

I tried to keep my mind off of it, though well-meaning friends kept calling to make sure that my grandmother hadn't been on that flight and I had to tell them that, actually, yes, Nonny had been blown to bits. I didn't put it that way, though part of me wanted to after answering the sixth such call.

Rowan called me Sunday around noon. "Are you still up to visiting Gretchen this week?"

"Yeah," I said. "Thursday still good for you?"

"Thursday's fine. I've done some sleuthing. She's home all the time, so I figured we can drive down in the morning and be back home before rush hour."

I stared at my calendar and suddenly, the numbers blurred. Woozy, I quickly sat down. I felt clammy, almost like I was breaking out in a cold sweat. "Hold on a minute." I took a couple deep breaths and then the dizziness cleared. "Thursday's fine for me. That will give me some time to get over the shock. How's Teran, really? She texted me to say she was all right."

"Shaken. She and her mother butted heads a lot. I think she could use some therapy to help her come to grips about the resolutions she'll never get from Naomi now. I'll pick you up at your house at nine AM on Thursday. We'll get to Seattle before noon that way."

"Nine it is. I'll see you then." I paused, then asked, "Do you think this will work?"

"I don't know," Rowan said. "But we can't wait for the perfect time—that may not arrive. We'll just have to go in with a wing and a prayer."

I jotted it down in my planner and then hung up. Thursday was just like any other day, except the fate of my future longevity rode on it—as did Teran's. Feeling vaguely nauseated, I cleaned until Ari arrived for the evening that we had planned a few weeks back. I hadn't told her yet about my grandmother's death yet, primarily because I didn't want her begging off. I needed my BFF right now.

"Well, Meagan and I have decided we're going to get pregnant," she said, breezing through the door with a sack containing popcorn, cola, and a couple boxes of malted milk balls.

For years in our teens, we spent every Friday night watching movies together, and we'd recently decided that, while we couldn't manage weekly movie-thons, we could plan a monthly movie marathon. Tonight we were set to binge watch *Chicago*, *Gypsy*, and *Cabaret*—approximately seven hours of music, women, and show biz. We were starting at five PM, and we'd order pizza for dinner around eight.

I sat down on the sofa, staring at her. "Really? When?"

"When did we decide or when are we going to?" Ari laughed.

"Both." I knew that Ari and Meagan wanted kids. Ari had wanted to wait but it sounded like Meagan's biological clock had been shrieking for months now.

"We made the decision last week. And we're both going to get complete physicals to decide who's in the best shape to carry a baby. We'll have to either find a sperm donor or sign up with a sperm bank. So I figure it should take about four or five months to lock down all the plans. At least it will be on our schedule and not an 'accident,' " she added, laughing.

Before I realized what I was doing, I let out a loud sigh. Ari and I had been best friends since we were kids, but more and more our lives seemed to be growing apart. First, Ari had gotten married, and now I was getting married, and soon she and Meagan would have children. I didn't want to lose what we had built up over the years, but everything evolved, and even if we grew apart, we'd still care about each other. But still, the thought made me even sadder than I already was.

"Something wrong?" Ari asked, her hand in the popcorn bowl.

I thought for a moment. I didn't want to spoil her news with my own reaction, and I didn't want to bring the evening to a halt. So I shook my head. "No, just...thinking. Let's watch the movie, okay?"

"Say, did Nonny get in? Where is she? With Teran?"

I wanted to ignore the question, but tears flecked my

eyelashes and I knew I'd have to tell her sometime. "Nonny's plane got…blown up by terrorists. She never made it here."

Ari dropped her cola on the floor as she bolted straight up. "What the hell? And you let me just barge in here, chatting about baby plans? When did this happened? Why didn't you call me?"

I hung my head. "I was afraid you might not come over—that you'd want to spare me company, but I need you to be here. I need the distraction."

"Tell me everything," Ari said as she threw a paper towel over the splattered soda on the floor and moved closer to take my hands in hers.

I told her what had happened.

"How horrible," Ari said. She worried her lip as she stared at me. "Is there anything I can do?"

"Just watch the movies with me. I need distraction. There's nothing else either of us can do right now." I paused, then added, "Congrats about your baby decision."

But Ari was onto me. "Hey, did that upset you, too? I can tell when something's off."

I stared at the remote in my hand. "No, I'm happy for you. But so many things have happened for both of us that it feels like what time we do have together has dwindled down to a moment here or there."

"Don't forget that the entire time you were married to Ellison was a big bite in our visits. You lived in Seattle, and he didn't like me." She adjusted herself on the sofa. "January, I don't like bringing this up, especially right now, but during that time you pretty much ignored me unless he was out of town and it was convenient to invite me down."

More tears welled up. I wanted to protest but she was telling the truth. I had been the one who fell down on the friend-front there. "I know…I know. It's just that Nonny's death has made me all too aware of how quickly everything can change. And right now, change doesn't feel very good. I'm really happy for you and Meagan, but I don't want to lose you." And for the first time since Esmara had told me the news, I burst into tears and really began to cry.

Ari scooted over to sit beside me, taking the remote out of my hand. She motioned for me to lie down with my head in her lap, and gently brushed her hand through my hair, rubbing my temples ever so slightly. I cried, ugly sobs bubbling up that I hadn't even realized were there.

"Talk to me," she said.

"My parents have only been gone a couple of years, and now Nonny is gone. And the curse is still active and I'm afraid I'll lose my aunt before we can break it. I don't want to lose anybody else. You've always been like my sister—and now…I have to share you and pretty soon, you'll be busy with your own family and—" I paused, feeling stupid. "Will there still be room for me in your life once you and Meagan have babies?"

"Of course there will. You and Killian still see Tally, right? And she has twins." Ari helped me as I sat up, sniffling and feeling like an idiot.

"Yeah, but…she's his family. She's kind of obligated to see us."

"Well, if I'm your sister in spirit, don't you think that I'll want to see you?" Ari shook her head and set the bowl of popcorn on the sofa. "I will always make time to see you. And you will always make time to see me. Because that's who we are. In fact, Meagan and I have already talked about it and we'd like you and Killian to be our children's godparents."

I tried to wipe my nose. "Really? You're not just trying to make me feel better?"

"Yes, I want you to feel better, but I'd never make a unilateral decision like that without talking to Meagan. We want you involved in our children's lives. I know you're not maternal, exactly, but I know you, January. And I like to think I know Killian by now. You're the ones we would trust the most." She grabbed a box of tissues from the end table. "I think that your grandmother's death affected you more than you realized."

I sat, cross legged, staring at my hands as I twisted the tissue. Finally, I blew my nose and then used a fresh tissue to wipe my eyes. I smeared my makeup but I didn't care.

"I think you're right. Though I do know I have worried about us growing apart. I'm sorry to dump all over you. I just…"

"I don't want us to grow apart, either. But we can't stay in limbo, and we're both on happy paths. Let's just make our own rules about this. Regardless of what any article out of *Glammed Out* or *Bling Ring* says, we don't have to grow apart just because we're moving on with our lives." She popped open a cola and handed it to me. I sipped it, grateful for the sharp metallic taste that cleared my sinuses.

"I'm all for that," I said, feeling worn out.

"You want to skip the movie binge tonight?"

I shook my head. "I'm tired but I want to just chill and forget about everything. Let's cut it down to two—*Chicago* and *Gypsy*. We can watch *Cabaret* later. It's depressing, anyway."

"Whatever you want," Ari said. "January—we'll always be best friends."

And when she said it, I knew she was telling the truth.

Monday morning, I felt a little more relaxed. The thought that, later this week, I'd be facing the witch who had been responsible for dooming the women of my family was daunting, but at least I'd have Rowan by my side. And Rowan wasn't afraid of anything.

Tad had made a more or less full recovery and was back in the office—he'd taken damage to his liver during our confrontation with Bigfoot, and had been hospitalized from June through September, then limited in mobility through the end of November. But he was allowed to return to work as long as he stayed at his desk and didn't try to fight anything.

He glanced at me, startled. I hadn't told anybody in the office about coming back to work yet, and they apparently either hadn't heard the news or made the connection between the flight and my grandmother.

"January, what are you doing here? You're supposed to be off with your grandmother."

I dreaded having to go over it yet once again, but they needed to know. I glanced around. Caitlin, Wren, and Hank were all here, so I called them over to the break table. Ever since we'd moved the office into a big old house that Tad had bought, everything seemed strange.

"Can everyone gather around? I have some news." I sat down, triple espresso latte in hand.

"What's going on?" Wren stared at me, then her eyes went wide. "Something's wrong. What happened?" She was as psychic as I was, and I could tell she'd picked up on something in my aura.

When everyone had settled in, I cleared my throat and brought out a pack of tissues. I could almost get through talking about it now without breaking down, but the constant repetition of the news was difficult.

"You know my grandmother was due in on Sunday, right?"

They nodded.

"I don't know if you saw the news about the Irish Isles airplane that was—"

"*Oh my gods,* your grandmother was aboard?" Wren froze in her chair, a horrified look on her face.

"Yeah, she was," I said, my throat strained.

"What happened? I was camping this weekend and didn't take my tablet." Hank looked alarmed.

"The United Freedom Liberation Front brought down a plane traveling from Ireland to the United States. They managed to stash a bomb on board in the cargo bay and my grandmother was sitting right over…" I stopped, unable to complete my thought.

Wren let out a cry and immediately was behind me, her arms around my shoulders, hugging me. "I'm so sorry, January."

As understanding spread over the others' faces, Tad grimaced, slapping his hand on the table. "You've got to be fucking kidding me." But his words weren't a question. He wiped his hands over his eyes. "I don't know what to say."

Caitlin sat, pensive, and Hank just stared at me with horror in his eyes.

"I couldn't stay home all week. I need to work. I need to sort through my thoughts while I'm busy doing something else. If I stay home, I'll go nuts. I will be gone Thursday, but otherwise, I want to work." I looked over at Tad, pleading for him to understand.

He gave me a slow nod. "If that's what you want, then of course. I'll cancel your time off except for Thursday. If you need more time, just ask. We're flexible."

"Thanks," I said, not knowing what else to say.

"Since we're already gathered, why don't you all grab your tablets and we'll get started for the day," he added. When we returned with our notebooks and tablets, Tad set a file folder on the table in front of him. "We have a new client. She was going to come in today, but events have escalated. So we're just going to meet her at her shop."

"What's the problem?" I tapped open the Notes app on my tablet and started a new list.

"Mella Jean Wilkes owns the Yoga Now studio. It's a yoga studio and crystal shop all rolled into one. She's been in the same location for ten years without incident but last week, things started happening and have escalated at an alarming rate. The first indication that something was wrong happened last Tuesday. The lights started turning on and off by themselves. She called an electrician that day, since she was afraid something had happened to the wiring. But he came out and took a look and he told her there was nothing wrong."

"I'm surprised she got somebody on the same day—that in itself is a miracle," Wren said.

"Yeah, well, she did and there was absolutely nothing that could have accounted for it. The electrician even saw it happen while he was there, but he looked all over and couldn't figure out what was causing it." Tad sucked on the inside of his cheek, creating an odd dimple. "The next day, she came in to find crystals on the ground, yoga mats sliced, all sorts of damage. She called the police and filed a report, but the door had been locked when she got there and she firmly remembered setting the security alarm before she left."

"Does she have security cameras, by any chance?" Caitlin asked.

"She didn't, but after a repeat on Thursday morning, a friend of hers came in and installed a couple. That's where things get wild. So, Saturday morning she opens the studio. By now she's spooked and has called off classes for the weekend, because she's not sure what's going on and all of her yoga mats were damaged. She finds the shop topsy-turvy again, so she calls her friend and he comes down and they look at the security footage. She forwarded me the digital footage."

Tad set up his laptop so we could all see it and pressed play.

The studio lights were off to start with, and we saw her leaving the shop, locking it up. A number of the shelves had been cleared.

"Did she take inventory off the shelves?" I asked.

Tad paused the film. "Yeah, she took her more expensive pieces home with her so they wouldn't get destroyed. Just watch." He started up the playback again.

As we watched, the lights suddenly turned on, illuminating the entire showroom. A second camera viewpoint angled into the studio practice room showed the lights in there blazing to life again as well. The next moment, in the main room, a picture flew off the wall, crashing to the floor. Crystals went flying around the shop, some of them landing against walls and shattering. A broom in the corner began to move through the room, whirling sideways in midair.

"Damn, that's one hell of a poltergeist she's got there," Caitlin murmured.

"Maybe," I said, the hairs on the back of my neck standing up. "But I don't think that's a poltergeist. Whatever it is, it feels…focused. Poltergeists are chaotic by nature."

I leaned forward, watching the footage as closely as I could, when a face appeared in the vortex, facing the camera. It reminded me of the face in the painting *The Scream*, warped like melted wax. The eye sockets were putrid green, like pus oozing out of a wound. The mouth was filled with razor-like teeth. I jumped and shrieked, so startled by its sudden appearance. The footage ended abruptly as the camera jostled and then fell. As it hit the floor, the images cut off.

"Crap!" Hank stared at the blank screen. "What the hell was that thing?"

"I don't know, but Mella hasn't been back to her studio since she downloaded the footage. She's too frightened to go back." Tad glanced over at me. "What do you think?"

"I don't know," I said. "Can you replay that at a slower speed so we can see the image more clearly?" I didn't really want to see the entity again, but we needed to figure out what we were dealing with here.

Tad obliged, freezing it at the point where the face appeared. There seemed to be no body attached to it—just the face coming out of the vortex, which resembled a tornado created by the mist. I studied it, trying to get some feel as to whether it was a ghost or not. There were plenty of other creatures around that weren't part of the spirit realm who liked to cause havoc.

"Thoughts?" I turned to the others. "Something tells me this might not be a spirit."

"You think we're dealing with a demon or some other astral nasty?" Caitlin asked. She was sitting next to Tad and I smiled as he reached out to pat her hand. I didn't think he even realized he was doing it. They had finally gotten together when Tad was hurt. It had jogged Caitlin into realizing that she might lose him, and she spent a lot of time in the hospital at his side. They meshed well together, and that they were making those little unconscious gestures of love spoke volumes as to how they were getting on.

I nodded. "Hold on, let me get my *Leafland's Compendium*."

Beside my desk stood a bookshelf, and I scanned through the titles until I found what I was looking for. I'd began gathering—thanks to a generous research budget from Tad—rare books on creatures from different realms. I was also scanning some of the old ones into PDFs so that if we ever had a fire, I'd still have them. Some of the books were incredibly expensive because they were so old and rare, and I wasn't about to let them fade into history. They were written before copyrights existed, and most of the authors were dead, so I wasn't breaking any laws.

Gerald Leafland had been a poet, but he had also been an

amateur ghost hunter back during the late 1800s. He had written a bestiary from his studies, and I had the only extant copy. Thanks to Tad's willingness to let me hunt through Net-Mart, the biggest online shopping co-op on the internet, I had managed to find it when it became available. *Leafland's Compendium* had cost us almost a thousand dollars, but it was worth it.

I carried the book back to the table. I had almost finished scanning the entire book, a good thing since some of the pages were so old the paper was beginning to crumble. As I gently thumbed through it, looking for something of which I had a vague memory, Hank stood and stretched.

"I think I'll make a coffee run. Anybody want anything?"

Even though we had an espresso machine in the kitchen of the house we were using as an office now, a new stand had opened just across the street. Leyla's Java Hut was home to the best-tasting coffee drinks that I'd ever had. I wasn't sure what her secret was, but we gave her more business than we probably should have.

"Triple-shot pumpkin spice latte, please," I said.

"Chai tea for me," Tad said. He'd taken up drinking tea more than coffee, given his liver injury.

Wren also ordered a chai tea, and Caitlin asked for a mocha. Hank pulled a twenty out of the petty cash box and headed outside. I watched him through the living room window—well, our main office window. The sky was brewing with heavy clouds, rolling in from the ocean, bringing with them yet another windstorm. The trail of storms that paraded across our area during October and November left massive winds and rain in their wake, causing urban and rural flooding, toppled trees, and regular power outages.

As I watched Hank dash across the street, a strange feeling began to steal over me. At first I thought it was about Nonny, but then realized that I was starting to feel a little woozy. On one hand, I felt like something was watching me, yet on the other—I couldn't feel any other presence, just this sense of impending doom. I glanced over my shoulder but Caitlin was working at her computer, Tad was poring over his planner, and Wren was filing a stack of old reports that had already been entered into the computer.

The oppressive feeling grew stronger, and I scanned the room, trying to pinpoint where the source was, but there was nothing I could actually point to. I decided to chalk it up to nerves and stress, but at that moment, a blinding jolt hit my temple and I moaned, wincing as I thought I might have heard someone whisper my name.

"What's up?" Tad asked, glancing up from his planner.

The pain backed off. I turned, studying the air closest to me, but again—I couldn't find anyone or anything there. My breath formed into puffs, though, as I asked, "Did one of you say something to me?"

Caitlin, Wren, and Tad shook their heads. Holding up my hand, I slowly turned to Caitlin.

"Can you get one of the FLIRs out and scan the area around me?"

Eyes wide, she nodded and ducked into our storeroom. Returning with the gadget, she held it out and turned it on, scanning the area where I was standing.

"Cripes. There's so much activity around you that I can't even get a clear reading, the needle's jumping like crazy. And the temperature around you is ten degrees cooler than the rest of the room." She motioned to Wren. "Grab an EVP, please."

As Wren vanished into the storeroom, Tad slowly approached me. I had a bad feeling about him coming closer and was about to wave him back when he went sprawling back on his ass.

"Tad!" I jumped forward, racing to where he was lying on his back, looking bewildered.

At that moment, Hank came through the door with our drinks. He immediately assessed the situation. Then, setting the drinks on the foyer table, he grabbed the EVP from Wren and—charging over into the living room—thrust it out in front of him.

"Whoever's there, make yourself known!"

But there was no response. The energy whirled and vanished, leaving us staring at one another with a million questions.

CHAPTER SIX

"What the ever-loving fuck?" I straightened up—I'd been about ready to dive under my desk. "What the hell was that?" I paused, then turned to Tad. "Are you all right? You took quite a tumble."

"I'm fine," he said, standing. "I need to avoid strenuous activity for now, but a tumble like that isn't going to break anything open."

"I don't know, but whatever it was, it was in your aura," Hank said to me. "Look at the readings on the FLIR." Caitlin had turned the infra-red device toward him, so he could see the temperature variations. "The temperature surrounding you was well over ten degrees lower than the rest of the room."

"I thought I heard it call my name," I said, staring at the FLIR. "I could be wrong, though. Wren, did we capture anything on the EVP?"

She handed it to Hank, who was much more proficient with it, and he plugged it into his massive computer array and flipped the switch to play the digital recording.

A deep, gravelly voice echoed out of the speakers. "You

can't get away from me. I know where you live. I know who you are." Then it cut off into maniacal laughter.

"Crap. What the fuck?" I leaned against the nearest chair, shivering. "What…who…that's not my Nonny, that I can tell you."

"You seem to have picked up a hitchhiker somewhere. Have you been around any haunted houses or cemeteries lately?" Tad frowned, a worried look on his face.

I shook my head. "No…wait, Killian and I went to a funeral the other night. I had the feeling I was being watched, but that's nothing new, given the way I can pick up on the dead." I sat down, trying to calm my breath. "Is he…it…whatever it is still here?"

Hank scanned the entire house with the FLIR. "No, whatever it is—whoever it is—seems to be gone now. I think we scared it away. But *you* need to beef up your wards. You can't allow astral nasties to cling onto you like that. Have you noticed anything else since the funeral—" He stopped, paling. "Of course you haven't, you've had other things to deal with."

I hung my head, wishing everything would just go back to normal. Everybody was worried about my feelings, and I valued that, but I also didn't like being the center of attention because of a tragedy. There was nothing I could do about Nonny. She was dead and over the Veil, and I was trying to figure out what my life would be without her. And sad to say, it wouldn't change drastically. I was more worried that the curse on my family was still in effect.

"I don't think I've noticed anything. I've had a headache off and on the past couple days, but that's not really much of a surprise, given what's happened. I'm tired, but I've just chalked it up to stress." My stomach lurched. Was the hitchhiker there when Killian and I made love? In many ways, the thought of an astral voyeur was as nerve-racking as one in the flesh, since I dealt with so many things on the other side.

Astral creatures were every bit as real as the people we interacted with every day.

"I guess all we can say is keep watch. Be alert, and if you sense this creature again, try to find out what it is. You most likely picked up a hitchhiker at the funeral home and now that he's had his fun, he's moved on," Hank said.

"Yeah, I guess so. I'm more highly attuned to the astral world right now, given Nonny's death, so maybe you're right. I still think you need to ward this house more, Tad. Because it was able to enter with me. Since you live upstairs, and we have a lot of sensitive material and equipment here, it's dangerous to leave it unguarded. I'd do it, but I'm worn out from the past few days, so you should hire a witch. Rowan can put you onto someone who's qualified." I returned to my desk. "Okay, should we head out to Mella's studio? It's only eleven."

Tad nodded, though he looked like he wanted to say something. But we gathered our things and, agreeing to take the van so we could all go together, headed out to visit the Yoga Now studio.

WHEN WE ARRIVED, MELLA WAS WAITING FOR US. I glanced around the studio and almost tripped over myself as I entered. The energy was so strong it made me dizzy. Not only was the crystal energy so strong it was humming, but whatever had taken up residence here was firmly entrenched. In fact, shadows were crawling across the walls where there shouldn't be any shadows, and I could hear a scraping that sounded like something dragging itself along in a dark basement.

"You don't have any other rooms besides the main room and the studio, do you?" I asked.

She pointed toward a door at the back of the room. "I have a small storeroom and a bathroom, also a cubbyhole that I use as a break room. There's just enough space for a microwave and mini-fridge."

"Can I take a look?" I wanted to see if the energy permeated the entire space.

She nodded. "Do whatever you need to."

"Caitlin, take a look next door on both sides. What shops does the studio buttress against?" I headed toward the back door and cautiously opened it. As I did so, a butter knife came whirling out, over my head, thankfully. It shot across the room and lodged firmly into the drywall. "Well, that's not very nice."

After the incident back at the office, I wasn't feeling all that generous. "Fucking knock it off, whoever the hell you are."

Apparently, my sentiments were not appreciated because behind me, Tad let out a yell. I whirled around just in time to see him ducking a quartz crystal spike that had come hurtling toward him. The crystal struck the opposite wall, then dropped to the floor.

"Cripes, thank you not." I turned back and strode into the break room area. The mini-fridge was open and its contents had been scattered on the floor. I turned and peeked into the bathroom. A bottle of liquid soap had been upended into the toilet, blocking the drain, and the handle was trying to flush it, but just causing a mess of bubbles to overflow. I grabbed the bottle and pulled it out, tossing it in the sink.

I finally opened the door to the storeroom. It was one of the tidiest, cleanest rooms I had ever seen in a store, except the few boxes that had been stored on the shelves were tipped over, their contents spilling onto the floor. There wasn't much there, at least, and I hoped none of it was expensive. I tried to get a read on the energy, but it wasn't sourced here. Instead, I followed the trail back to the main room, where it grew stronger.

"I have no—" I stopped, staring across the room. There, sitting on one of the counters, was a mask that immediately pulled me in. The mask itself was abstract, but the energy around it was chaotic, like a whirling dervish, spinning out from the center. I walked over to the mask and sat down in a chair beside it. It was carved from some sort of softwood, and had been painted and stained. There weren't distinct features on it, but symbols that I couldn't read.

"What's this?" I asked.

Mella glanced over at me. "A Coyote mask. He's the—"

"I know who Coyote is," I said. "What do these symbols mean?"

She shrugged. "I don't know. I found the mask in the bottom of a basket, actually. Somebody left it in the shop, and I kept it in the lost and found box for three months, but nobody ever returned looking for it. There was nothing to identify who it belonged to, so I decided to set it out so it might trigger someone into remembering they had left it here. It's lovely but sometimes it makes me uneasy."

"Yeah, I understand why," I said. The mask made me uneasy, too. In fact, it repelled me. There was something twisted about it, something so chaotic it left me feeling queasy, as though if I watched it long enough, maggots might crawl out from the eyeholes.

"You picking up something?" Hank asked, bringing the FLIR over.

"Yeah, I think so. Check out the mask."

He did, then caught his breath. "Come look at this," he said.

I moved around to stand beside him. There, on the monitor of the FLIR, I could see massive worms crawling around the mask, and a moth hovering over it.

"Cripes, not Mothman again," I muttered.

"No, I don't think so. Those look like argenium worms. They're astral creatures who feast on decaying energy, and the residue often acts like a poltergeist. I saw something similar once, years ago. The mask infects highly energetic places so that the energy decays—becomes moldy or putrid. The worms eat the energy, then when they transform into moths, they fly away. They work synergistically. Argenium worms aren't evil, but they embody chaos and they embody turmoil. The more, the better." He turned back to the mask.

"Can we kill them?" Tad joined us.

"We can, but not with anything we have here." Hank motioned to me. "This is your arena, January. We need holy graveyard dirt, some lacerium powder, and I'm not sure what else."

"Looks like I'm going to have to make a trip to the Broom & Besom." I was learning herbal magic from my aunt Teran—far later than I should have, but at least we were working on it. Rowan was scheduled to start teaching me the magic belonging to death and spirits, but we hadn't had a chance to really dive in. "Should we leave the mask here?"

"What's going on?" Mella asked. "Did you say something is wrong with the mask?"

"Yes, it's infested with some astral moths that are causing havoc in your store. The mask is poisoning the energy here, and then the worms eat it and turn into moths. I think." I paused. "Do I have that right?"

Hank nodded. "That's the simplest explanation. The fact that the mask has Coyote's energy is coincidental. The mask itself is a problem—not the deity it represents. The moths have nothing to do with Coyote. They're the ones causing the poltergeist activity, but it's incidental, not a primary focus."

"I'm not sure I understand," she said.

"Think about this way: you have some weed. Somebody

sneaks in and laces it with crack. Smoke the weed that hasn't been tainted and you get pleasantly high, maybe even a little psychedelic jaunt. But if you smoke the crack-laced weed, you have a really bad trip."

At that, she nodded. "I see what you're saying. So, somehow the mask got laced and the worms love it?"

"That's the best way I can describe it," Hank said. "January, can you run over to the Broom & Besom?"

I glanced at my watch. It was nearly noon. "They should be open now. I'll meet you…where?"

"Meet us at Lucky's Diner. We'll eat lunch downtown. Maybe we can clear the shop this afternoon." Tad turned to Mella. "Would you join us for lunch?"

She nodded. "Thanks. I just hope I don't have to get rid of everything in the shop."

As I headed out, I realized that I'd have to catch a cab, since I hadn't brought my car. Luckily, there was an old-fashioned taxi stand near the marina, and I headed over toward it. Yoga Now was located on the main drag in town.

Moonshadow Bay's town square was lovely, especially during the autumn and winter months. Pumpkins decorated most of the shops in town along with Samhain décor, and there was a general feeling of celebration in the air.

A shadow town, Moonshadow Bay straddled worlds—with footholds into the world of spirit, the world of the Fae, and the world to other mysterious places. One of three shadow towns that I knew of in Washington state, Moonshadow Bay was by far the most congenial. Whisper Hollow was dark and haunted, while Terameth Lake seemed a bit lighter, even with a local wilderness area known as Hell's Thicket. Moonshadow Bay was more magical than the latter, more inviting than the former.

It was stormy enough that I chose to pay a taxi driver to drive me the six blocks to the Broom & Besom. The magic shop was located between Mab's Bakery, catering to the allergic and gluten-free crowd, and Tucker's Fitness, an odd but fun gymnasium that I worked out in. I was still considering whether to sign up for one of Tucker's wilderness survival courses, but each time I started to go in to talk to him about it, I ended up turning around and going to Mab's Bakery for a cupcake instead.

As I pushed through the doors to the magic shop, Lisette greeted me. She was dusting off a shelf of jars filled with various herbs. Lisette and her wife Sira owned the shop, and they were aquanistas—powerful water witches. I suspected at times they actually went down to calm the waters in the bay when ships were in danger. They had recently returned from a world cruise, and I noticed a few new items around the shop that they must have brought back with them. One, an adorable bag in the shape of the hatbox, appealed to me but I already had a bag for my magical gear and I really didn't need to spend another hundred dollars on a new one.

"January! How good to see you," Lisette said, coming over and taking my hands. "How is everything? How are the wedding plans going?"

It seemed like everybody around town knew about my wedding, although I knew that was an exaggeration. But word got around. Moonshadow Bay wasn't particularly tiny, but it was small enough so that people easily could find out about anybody else's business if they wanted.

"Well, while you were gone I ended up buying a haunted wedding dress. I'm not sure what to do with it now. It's beautiful, but I don't feel like I can wear it without thinking about the bride who was murdered in it. I ended up helping her spirit sever ties with the dress, so that's something. Oh, and Killian's sister had her babies. Tally had twins. She named them Victoria and Leanna and they were born at the end of July."

"Oh, isn't that wonderful. Hopefully, mother and children are both happy and healthy? As far as you and the dress, let me think if I have anything that might help."

I glanced around the shop. "I'm kind of in a hurry or I'd stop to talk longer. I need some holy graveyard dirt, and lacerium powder. I don't know what else. We're dealing with argenium worms and moths. We need to destroy an infestation."

"Argenium worms? Oh dear. Those can be nasty to deal with and they're not easy to eradicate. I definitely have holy graveyard dirt, and I think I have some lacerium powder in the back. But those two alone won't do the trick. Give me a moment. If you want, have a seat over in the corner. Nobody's coming to read tarot for a while." She disappeared behind a set of curtains behind the counter.

I settled at the table, still looking at the hatbox. It was absolutely gorgeous. It looked as though it was made of leather, but the scene painted on it was one of flowering irises in front of the Eiffel Tower. The painting was reminiscent of Monet, and it brought to mind his *Water Lilies* painting.

A moment later Lisette returned, a basket over her arm filled with items. She sat beside me and began pulling them out, one by one. A plastic bag, firmly zipped, was filled with dirt. "Two ounces of graveyard dirt, which will be more than you need. It's been cleansed and blessed. And here is the lacerium powder." She placed a small plastic bag on the table. It contained about an ounce of a white, shimmering, holographic powder.

"What *is* lacerium powder?" I asked. I had never heard of it before.

"The natural enemy of the argenium worm is an astral wasp-like creature called the lacerium. It will sting the argenium and plant its eggs inside of the worm, as long as it hasn't managed to make it to the moth stage yet. The eggs quicken and then hatch inside of the worm and eat it from the inside out. But powdered lacerium wings can also poison the argenium worm."

I shuddered. "Nature can be nasty on both sides of the astral plane, can't it?"

"Definitely. Big Mama doesn't pull her punches. Now, sprinkling these on the worms would kill them if there were only a couple. But if you have an infestation, chances are you're not going to find all the eggs. So you're going to need a few other items. This," she held up a bottle, "is a combination of war water and a psychic disinfectant. Sira and I make it, and it is guaranteed to take care of most lowest-level demons. Argenium worms are considered demonic, although they aren't anywhere as nasty as most of the other demons. They're more like a demon insect." She paused, then asked, "Where is this infestation?"

"In a yoga studio. There was some crystals and other New Age items around, a few magical things. The vibration level of the shop is fairly high, so it surprised me that the argenium worms got a hold there."

"It doesn't surprise me at all," Lisette said. "Argenium worms are among the most tenacious of the astral insects. I have actually seen them manage to gain a foothold in a Greek temple before and that's not easy to do, especially when you're dealing with a goddess like Athena."

She chuckled. "Now, there are two other things you'll need. First, you will go in with the mixture of the graveyard dirt and the lacerium wings and sprinkle it on every single argenium worm or moth that you can see. Next, spray the combination of war water and disinfectant around the entire shop. I don't mean that you have to get droplets on every single inch of every wall, but you need to clear out the corners and nooks and crannies. After twenty-four hours, you'll go back with this." She held out a bottle of gunky green water.

"What's that? It looks disgusting."

"In one sense it is, because it's made out of slugs, squid, and several other creatures that most people don't care for. It's drawn off of their auras and run through a condenser, and then refined. This is one of the most potent purification mixtures you will ever encounter. It's extremely expensive, but I guarantee it will work."

I stared at the bottle. It was barely big enough to hold an ounce of liquid. "And that's for the entire shop?"

"And more. It's a concentrate. If you add this to a gallon of water, you'll have the correct proportions. You will then spray the entire shop with this product. On the third day—twenty-four hours after the spraying—go in, cast the circle, and light this incense. Let it smoke for fifteen minutes. And that should take care of your problem."

As she replaced everything in the basket, I thought it took a remarkable amount of energy just to ward off a few bugs, astral or not. Lisette sat back in her chair, waiting.

"Well, that's certainly complicated enough. I've written everything down, so I should have the proper instructions." I sat back, contemplating the basketful of components. "So, what's this going to run me?" Luckily, I had the company credit card with me. I couldn't imagine that something like the purification liquid would be cheap.

"Everything in this basket is going to cost you a total of $375. I'm sorry it's so expensive, but lacerium wings run dear. They're difficult to find, and procuring them brings its own dangers." She flashed me a sympathetic smile.

I handed her the credit card. "Is there any timing that is important for this—phases of the moon, planets aligning, anything like that?"

"No. Just make certain that you complete it in three

stages, with at least twenty-four hours between each stage. You may notice activity picking up during the actual clearing process. That's normal."

"How do they spread? Can you accidentally carry them to other places?"

"They can lay their eggs on anything, especially anything porous. Usually they can't get a foothold in the harder crystals like quartz, but if it's under a six on the Mohs hardness scale, there's a good chance that they've managed to lay eggs in there."

I groaned. "That means she'll have to change the carpeting, all the yoga mats, all the bolsters, some of the crystals—oh, hell, she's taken home some of the more expensive items, so if any of them are porous—"

"She'll have to cleanse her home as well. She can clean the carpeting and everything, but it's just going to be a lot of work. And anybody who's been in the shop since the argenium worms arrived might have carried out eggs on their purchases."

That brought up a thought. "What about us? The crew? We were only there an hour or so. Is there a way we can find if any of us have eggs clinging to our clothes? And what about your shop?" I suddenly imagined a trail of argenium eggs scattered around the town. "I came here in a taxi..."

"If your clothes have any eggs on them, there's a chance the cab could have been infected. Given the larvae are still milling around and they aren't all moths yet, that means there are probably unhatched eggs in her shop. And given you saw at least one moth, that means that there's a possibility more eggs have been laid. I'd better lay in a good store of supplies because this won't end at the yoga studio. There's not much you can do except change clothes before you go home and treat the ones you're wearing. Don't take them into your house." She shook her head. "We haven't had an infestation of argenium worms in a couple of decades."

"What am I supposed to do? Walk around town naked? I can't very well walk into a dress shop and potentially spread contamination, in case I have eggs on me. Did you say whether there was a chance that we can determine what's been infected and what hasn't?"

"I was about to, dear, if you'd let me get to it. I do have a tool that works—and it's something you can easily pick up at any marijuana shop. A blacklight will show the eggs. There's something about them that the UV light picks up on, just like it shows up scorpions. I have one in the back. Wait here, and we can inspect you." She hustled into the back as I contemplated the possibility of heading home naked in my car. How would I ever explain that to the cops, who would surely pull me over?

Lisette returned with a flashlight that had an odd purple light. I remembered my mother and father talking about blacklights in their college days, but I had never thought about getting one. Now, though? The idea seemed comforting.

She bade me stand up and slowly turn as she carefully ran the light over my clothes. I took off my jacket so we could examine every inch. Then, relieved that she had cleared my outer clothing of being infested, she made me go with her into the back where I took off my skirt and sweater, and she checked out my bra and panties and socks.

"You're clear. You shouldn't walk back into that shop without wearing protection, though. Some time back, the Court Magika worked with a group of researchers to create a magical hazmat suit. Made out of an olefin material that's spunbonded with polypropylene, the resulting product is then infused with magical barriers to create a suit that cannot be penetrated by creatures like argenium eggs." She dug through a closet and brought out a suit that looked like it was plague resistant.

I stared at her as I fingered the material. It felt strong and impenetrable under my fingers. "I had no idea that magic and technology were fusing together like that."

"Oh, the things going on now would knock your jaw out. You can borrow the suit till you finish cleaning the shop. I recommend you wear just your birthday suit inside it, though, just for extra protection. While the suits are resistant to being gashed or torn, they aren't foolproof."

I held up the UV flashlight. "Can I borrow this until I can buy one? I want to check out the rest of the crew, as well as Mella—the owner of the shop."

"Sure. Just bring it back when you're done with it, along with the suit. If you have any questions, give me a call."

With that, I gathered up my purchases and the suit and—relieved that I wasn't packing any of the creepy-ass worms or eggs on me—I headed outside to hail another taxi.

CHAPTER SEVEN

"You have to be kidding!" Tad stared at me as I ordered them all out of the diner where they were still waiting for food.

"I'm not. I need to pat you down with a blacklight, for lack of a better word." I paid the bill and, keeping my distance just in case one of the others was infected, made them follow me outside and across the street to a small park. We wouldn't be so obvious there. As I began to examine each of them with the UV flashlight, I filled them in on what I had learned. "I know far more about argenium worms than I ever wanted to know," I added.

Hank was fascinated. Caitlin looked mildly horrified. Tad's eye twitched. Mella grimaced and began to scratch.

"I hate bugs," she said. "Please don't tell me they're on me."

"If they are, you need to know. They won't attack your skin, but they spread." I ran the blacklight over each one of them in turn. Tad had a couple of the worms in his aura, but Caitlin was clear and so was Hank. But Mella's aura was so infested I almost gasped. "Have you been feeling listless the past couple of days?"

She nodded. "Yeah, I have."

"No wonder. Your aura's filled with eggs. They're probably tainting your energy."

"What do I do? I can't stand the thought of them leeching off me!"

"We'll take care of it. Okay, Caitlin, Hank, back away. I don't want the worms jumping on you. But…I need to go inside the van to change." I felt awkward, but I didn't want to chance any of the worms making a getaway to me.

"You're changing clothes *now?*" Hank stared at me.

I held up the bag with the suit in it. "Magical hazmat suit. Lisette lent it to me."

Hank walked me over to the van and I crawled in, making sure I wasn't in view of the front windshield. I sat on the floor, stripped everything off—including my bra—and folded my clothes on one of the chairs by the bank of computer equipment. Then I slid inside the hazmat suit. Since I was going commando, I'd call Lisette about how to clean it before returning it. I didn't want to leave any coochie cooties or scent in the suit. That would just be nasty. I fastened the hood to the neck of the suit and, to my relief, realized there was a filter through which I could breathe outside air, other than my own natural BO.

I knocked on the door and Hank opened it, helping me down. He stifled a laugh. "You look like you're expecting a plague."

"Don't laugh," I muttered. "It's happened before, it can happen again. Okay, Tad and Mella, please enter the shop but stand right near the door."

Carrying all the supplies—which were a bit unwieldy—I followed them inside. I prepared the holy graveyard dirt and the lacerium powder and, using the UV light to pinpoint where the worms were, I dusted the creatures with a thin coating of both. The worms froze, then immediately bounced off of Tad and Mella. I quickly sprayed them with the combination of war water and psychic disinfectant. After I finished, I motioned for them to hurry back outside.

"That should take care of them," I muttered, shining the UV light around. The worms were easy to find with it, but there were a lot of them and the eggs were even more numerous. The moths seemed to know what I was up to and tried to fly out of reach but I went after them first, tossing a fine stream of graveyard dirt and lacerium powder after them. The combo grounded them. I sprayed them with the war water mixture, just to be safe, and they seemed to melt like slugs when you sprinkled salt on them.

Heartened, next I went after the worms and eggs. I poked in every cubbyhole and crevice, searching out any that might be trying to hide. It took me two hours, but by the time I was done, the shop was covered with a thin layer of the dust, and I had melted every freaking worm in there. Then I doubled down, spraying every corner of the shop with the war water and disinfectant.

When I was done, I found a mirror and ran the blacklight over myself. No worms. I was safe to go back outside. As I came out of the door, I found the others sitting on the benches outside the Yoga Now studio, looking concerned.

"We're done for twenty-four hours," I told them. "Then I need to come back and spray your shop with another disinfectant. And twenty-four hours after that, I have yet another ritual to perform and then it should be good. But there's a problem. Anybody who's been in your shop the past—well, however long you've had the worms—has the potential to be infected. So we're going to have to let the authorities know, because they could be anywhere in the city."

"Is there a citywide ritual we can perform to remove them in one blanket sweep?" Tad asked.

"I don't know. Lisette knew quite a bit about these creatures. We can ask her, or maybe my grandmother Rowan will know." As I said the word *grandmother* I felt a thud inside.

During the work to remove the worms, I had managed to put the memory of Nonny's death out of my mind, but now it came roaring back. I drew my hand across my forehead. I hated when the shadows swept in. Being busy kept them at bay. Focusing on other things kept them at arm's length. But when I was done, and had a moment to breathe, they came rushing back to envelop me again. I seldom suffered from depression, though the eighteen years with Ellison had been a massive mood-drain, but sharp losses—like death—were enough to tank anybody.

I let out a sigh. "I'll be back tomorrow. Do you have your purse? I don't suggest going in there again until I finish. Just lock up and leave it alone."

"I have my things. Can you check them for the worms?" Mella held out a backpack.

I motioned for her to open it and scanned it with the blacklight. "It's clean, it looks like. Go home and meet me here tomorrow at two PM." I headed back to the van, where I checked it for eggs too, and found it was also clean. "Let me change clothes first. I don't fancy riding back to the office in this."

Hank opened the door for me and I climbed inside, quickly changing as soon as the door closed. After that, we headed back to the office. I left the hazmat suit in the van, returning it to the bag. The bag itself was also made out of the same material, so it wouldn't leech anything out into its surroundings.

BACK AT THE OFFICE, I STARED AT MY COMPUTER, IN NO mood to write up a report.

"You okay, January?" Tad asked.

"What?" I turned around, blinking.

"I've asked you three times if you were okay and you didn't answer." He frowned. "Are you sure you want to be here?"

"What am I going to do if I go home? Sit there and focus on Nonny exploding over the water? That's not exactly an enticing prospect, you know." Taking a deep breath, I calmed myself down. Tad wasn't to blame for any of this and he didn't deserve to get caught in the crosshairs. I let out a long sigh. "I'm sorry. I don't mean to snap…it's just…everybody keeps asking how they can help, or shouldn't I be resting, but I don't want to rest. When I rest, I have time to think and right now, I don't want to go into the dark spaces where my thoughts are."

He gave me a nod. "I get it. Tell you what, write that up later. I have another case pending. Why don't you interview the couple? They'll be here in twenty minutes. Their house is haunted and they're looking for answers. I haven't done an intake interview on them, so why don't you handle it?"

I shrugged. "I can do that. It will also give me some feel for who they are and how much of what they're telling us is bogus."

A number of would-be debunkers had started coming in, supposedly with terrifying cases. But they were just trying to disprove our work so they could prove to the world that we were scammers. We'd never been caught by one yet, and in fact, we'd changed the mind of several hardcore skeptics, but they were never a joy to work with and the sooner we spotted them, the less time we wasted.

"Use the den to talk to them. Here's the initial file." He handed me a folder. I carried it back to my desk and opened it. Inside were their names and address, and a brief summary of their call.

Terry and Brenda Shoner had recently moved to town and bought a new house. They had no sooner moved in when they began hearing noises from the attic at night, like something heavy dragging across the floor. This continued for a week or two, and they had initially written it off as squirrels or some other critter that had gotten trapped up in the attic. But when Terry went up to check, he had found nothing there except a few pieces of furniture—a rocking chair, an old bookcase with a few nondescript books in it, and an old empty trunk.

That night, the footsteps had escalated into pounding, and they heard grunts and groans. Brenda had insisted on calling the police, but the cops found nothing when they checked out the house. They suggested maybe the neighbors were loud, but according to the couple, the nearest neighbors were eighty if they were a day, and their lights were out by nine PM every night.

"Have we looked into the background of the house yet?" I asked.

Tad shook his head. "No, I decided to wait until they actually hired us. But if we take them on, then you can start the research into that as well, if you like."

I nodded. "Fine with me." The busier I was, the less time I had to mull over events. A few moments later the couple showed up, the fear immediately apparent on their faces. I led them into the den and asked them to sit down.

"Tad says you're having problems with a ghost?" I held up a digital recorder. "Do you mind if I record our session? Unless there's something illegal on it, I guarantee it will go no further than our office without your permission."

Brenda glanced at Terry, who nodded. "All right."

I set the recorder up and then I stated the date, "October 16," gave the year and time, and then repeated my question.

"Yes, I think it's a ghost. I don't know what else it could be. It starts every night around nine-thirty. We haven't heard it during the day, until yesterday." Brenda reeked of fear, and it wasn't the fear of being caught in a lie. I could sense it rolling off of her.

"Excuse my question, but you and Terry—you're *human*, right?"

She nodded. "We moved to Moonshadow Bay because our best friends live here, and we wanted to get out of the city. It was always so pretty when we came to visit that we decided to move here. I don't know if you know them—Vern and his wife Melony LaFoy? He's a bear shifter who owns an urban farm on the outskirts of town."

I shook my head. "No, I haven't had the pleasure of meeting them. Why don't you tell me what happened when you found the house? Did you sense anything odd when you were first looking at it?"

She shook her head. "Neither one of us considers ourselves to be psychic. Oh, I've had my cards read a couple of times and the readings were right on point, and I believe in ghosts because my mother used to tell me stories about how her father watched over her even after he died. She'd wake up and he'd be sitting by her bed at night, keeping an eye on her. Not in a creepy way, but—" Brenda paused, sighing. "I mean..."

"I understand. He was acting like a guardian—standing sentinel?"

She nodded. "Right. He was devoted to his family. Anyway, so I never met my grandfather, but I believed my mother."

"How about you?" I asked Terry. "Do you believe in ghosts?"

"I don't *dis*believe in them. I thought I was neutral on the subject until we moved into the house. Now, I just want to know what the damn thing is and I want it out. I don't like being scared of my own home." He sounded a little belligerent, but that was understandable. Nobody liked to think their home was being invaded.

"All right. How long after you moved in before the activity began?"

"Two days. The second night, actually." Terry frowned. "I woke up during the night and heard something overhead in the attic. I figured it was squirrels or something. I woke Brenda up and pointed out the noise to her, because I wanted to remember to hire pest control to come and check it out the next day. I'm new to home repair and I want to leave things to the experts, including unwanted guests."

I was jotting down notes as they talked. We used the digital recordings to make sure we didn't miss anything, but it also helped to note down expressions, body language, and so forth. Our clients didn't seem to realize that's what we were doing. Right now, both of them looked on edge, with Terry a little more angry than Brenda. Brenda looked tired, with bags under her eyes, and it was my guess they weren't normally there. They seemed to be an active couple, physically fit. That could be misleading, but it was a place to start.

"You're missing sleep, right?"

Brenda nodded. "The noises started every single night after nine-thirty. A sliding sound, almost a hissing. Occasionally, I think I can hear shouting but when I try to focus on them, they vanish. We called the pest control company, but they couldn't find anything up there. No squirrels, no birds, no bats—nothing. We called the cops the next night, but they couldn't find any sign of anything anywhere, and there were no signs any windows had been tampered with. I think they thought we were drunk, because they suggested that the neighbors were causing the noise. I like the Whimsys, but they go to bed at nine every night, and while they're polite, they keep to themselves."

"What happened yesterday? You said things began to escalate?" Usually hauntings *did* escalate, especially if the people living in the house started to renovate, or if they tried to evict the unwanted visitors. "Did you do anything out of the ordinary yesterday?"

Brenda blushed. She gave me a half-shrug. "Well, I tried to sage the house. I know that it's supposed to help, so I bought a sage stick and went through the house, ordering whatever was there to leave. That's when the picture flew off the wall and crashed at my feet."

Okay then, we were getting around to overt paranormal activity. But I had the feeling that whatever they were dealing with wasn't a poltergeist. That usually started out with items moving. "Was that all that happened?"

Brenda shook her head. "No, actually, I hate to say it but I think I made things worse. Not only did the picture come off the wall, but my favorite crystal figurine flew off the shelf and shattered at my feet. I jumped, and when I did, I heard something hissing at me. I called Terry to come home from work and we went to a hotel. That's when we called Vern and told him what was going on. He recommended we call you guys. So this morning we did."

"Have you been back to your house since last night?"

Terry shook his head. "No. I didn't want to go in without any guidance. There's obviously something there that wants us out and I have no clue what to do."

"The saging didn't work, that much was clear." Brenda glanced at me, looking vaguely guilty. "I shouldn't have tried that, should I?"

"It's not necessarily a bad idea, and with negative energy that's just accumulated or that's minor in nature, it can work just fine. But when you're dealing with a haunting and you have no training, it tends to stir things up even worse." I sat back, glancing over the page of notes I'd taken. They were for real, that much I could tell, and they were frightened. "Let me go talk to Tad. I'll be right back." I turned off the recorder and pocketed it, then closed the door behind me, walking over to Tad's desk.

"Well?" he asked.

"They're for real, and they need help. I'd like to take the case. We should do a walk-through as well as dig out information on the house. The haunting is starting to escalate. From what they told me, I don't think we're dealing with a simple poltergeist." I shrugged. "What kind of a quote should I give them?"

"Let's make it five hundred to start—for an assessment and research. Don't guarantee we can fix the problem, and that isn't included under the initial fee. But we'll do our best to determine what's going on and what the easiest way is to solve the issue."

I returned to the den and laid out the plan to them. "We'll be doing extensive research into the house and land, what was there before the house, who lived there and who died there, and I'll come out and do a walk-through. I'm witchblood, and I specialize in both earth energy and working with the dead, so I should be able to get a grasp on what you're facing."

Brenda glanced at Terry, who nodded. "Do you have a payment plan? We spent most of our money on the move and don't have a lot of cash lying around."

We often worked with clients who weren't well off or who needed longer times to pay. "Yes, we do. We have an interest-free monthly payment plan, as long as you keep current. Can you manage fifty dollars a month, with fifty up front?" I began to fill in the information on their intake form.

Terry let out a sigh of relief. "That's perfect. I can put a hundred down, if that will help. And fifty a month is perfect." He pulled out his wallet and brought out five twenty-dollar bills. I wrote him out a receipt and we agreed on the fifth of each month for their payment due. That gave him time to deposit his paycheck. We set up an automatic deduction from his bank account.

"When we determine how much it's going to cost for the solution—hopefully it won't be too much—then we can refinance the contract. Please sign here." I pushed the contract over to their side of the desk. They read it, then signed.

"When can you come out to the house?"

I glanced at the clock. It was three-thirty. I didn't feel like going home early, but the best time for me to visit would be in the evening. Especially since the activity usually started around nine PM. "We can come over tonight. I'll need one of you—or both, if you like—to be there. We'll bring our equipment and set up surveillance. Hank and Caitlin will probably be with me, at least." I always specified that I wouldn't be alone. There were too many stories about women being lured to their death on the internet and they were impossible to ignore.

We made arrangements and I walked them out, stopping by Tad's desk to introduce them to the others. "We need to set up equipment at their house tonight. Caitlin, Hank, you game?"

Hank nodded. "The only date I had tonight was with my sofa and the newest episode of *House Squad*."

Caitlin glanced at Tad, who nodded. "I can be there. I don't have any plans."

I knew they had just broken a date. "Hey, if you guys—"

"No, we'll both be there," Tad said. "I'm feeling up to it. So we'll see you tonight, Terry and Brenda. Please don't go inside till we get there. If things are escalating, we don't want you getting hurt. And do you have a place to stay in the meanwhile? The activity can get ugly during the time we're investigating."

"We can't afford the hotel much longer—it's draining us dry," Terry said. "I'll call Vern and see if he and Melony will let us stay at their house. They have a guest cottage on the farm." He stepped away to make a phone call and then returned, relief shining through his eyes. "We can stay there. But we'll need to pack our bags tonight, since we only took a few things when we left the other day."

"Good. We'll see you there tonight at eight-thirty. Now go have dinner and don't worry—we'll do our best to get you all squared away." I escorted them out and then returned. "Whatever is haunting their house, it's not happy. She tried saging it out and that didn't go well at all."

"Well, I guess we'll find out what's going on tonight," Tad said, grinning.

"Yeah, I guess we will," I said. But I didn't feel like smiling. The energy around the couple was heavy and loomed over me. I returned to my desk, staring at my coffee cup. My head hurt, and I wondered if I should just go home and take a nap.

CHAPTER EIGHT

We got our equipment ready to go and decided to take a four-hour break, then regroup at eight to gather our gear and head out to the Shoners' house. On my way home, I stopped at the House of Dragons and picked up some fried rice, potstickers, egg rolls, and orange chicken. By the time I arrived home, it was four-thirty. I texted Killian.

I STOPPED AND PICKED UP CHINESE FOR DINNER. I HAVE TO GO OUT AGAIN AROUND EIGHT. WE HAVE A NEW CASE AND I NEED TO DO A WALK-THROUGH TONIGHT. WHEN WILL YOU BE HOME?

A few moments later, he texted back. I'LL BE LATE TONIGHT—WE HAVE TWO EMERGENCY CASES AND BOTH OF US NEED TO BE THERE. THE TECHS ARE PREPPING THE DOGS RIGHT NOW. NASTY FIGHT—A DOBERMAN AND A ROTTY GOT INTO IT, AND YOU CAN IMAGINE HOW BAD IT IS. I HATE IT WHEN OWNERS CHOOSE BREEDS THAT CAN BE DANGEROUS AND WON'T PUT THEIR DOGS THROUGH TRAINING. CHANCES ARE THE DOBERMAN'S GOING TO LOSE A LEG AND THE ROTTY MIGHT LOSE AN EYE.

Killian's vet practice was thriving, but he hated coping with stupid people. He'd recently hired a second vet to take some of the load off, and Mike was as good as they came.

CRIPES, THAT SOUNDS NASTY. I'LL BE LEAVING AROUND TEN MINUTES TO EIGHT, SO I'LL PUT THE REST OF THE FOOD IN THE FRIDGE FOR YOU. I DON'T KNOW WHEN I'LL BE HOME, BUT TEXT ME WHEN YOU GET OFF AND I'LL HAVE A BETTER ESTIMATE OF WHEN YOU SHOULD EXPECT ME. LOVE YOU.

LOVE YOU TOO.

I set my phone down on the table and dished out half the food onto a plate, then closed the containers and tucked them into the fridge. Then, curling up on the sofa, I turned on the TV. The news was on and—of course—there was more about the plane crash. I sighed.

You aren't going to get away from it, Esmara said, showing up next to the television.

I had ceased being startled when she appeared. "I wish I could. I didn't realize this was going to hit me so hard and, oh my gods, I should check on Teran. I haven't called her today." Feeling like pond scum, I grabbed my phone.

Your aunt is resilient. She will have some baggage to deal with, but she's quite capable of handling matters. Prue is with her, and she'll help. Meanwhile, what are you and Rowan doing about the curse?

"We're planning on heading down to Seattle on Thursday. I need to contact her and ask how she knows Gretchen will be home. I think we're mostly going to try to get a feel for who we're dealing with. Gretchen's been alive for a long time, and I'm hoping that if Val Slater talks to her, she'll just give in and break the curse." To be honest, I wasn't sure what we'd do if she didn't. Rowan and I hadn't talked it through that far yet.

"The plane went down with one hundred and five people aboard and no one is thought to have survived. All families have been notified. Authorities have not verified whether the United Freedom Liberation Front actually committed the bombing yet, but Wilder Cole of the National Transportation Safety Board has assured the public that they are on the case, and since this took place in international waters, the AAIB—the Air Accidents Investigation Branch—is spearheading the investigation. The two agencies are working together on an international basis to discover what really happened to Flight 1182. Forty-three Americans were aboard, two Canadians, and sixty-five Irish citizens."

The commentator was altogether too perky and cheerful for my taste. I turned off the television. "Do you really think that Gretchen's curse caused that plane to crash?" I asked.

Esmara shook her head. *No, it didn't actually cause the crash. But I do believe it caused Naomi to book a flight on it. That's the thing, January. A curse doesn't necessarily* cause *an* event, *but it can cause someone to end up being* part *of the event.*

I sighed. "I wish that I could quit thinking about this. I love Nonny, I really do. And I miss her, but—I didn't really know her that well. Why is it hitting me so hard?"

Death affects us in ways we don't expect. Sometimes we're able to just shoulder it and move on, and other times—it cuts like a knife. I suspect you feel some sort of guilt over the fact that she was coming to visit you.

"I think you're right. If she hadn't been coming to see me, then she wouldn't have been aboard that plane."

Ah, but that's not necessarily accurate. She might have decided to come visit Teran. Or she might have ended up in a car crash instead, or she might have gone out walking and fallen over the edge of a cliff. Who knows what might have happened? But if it was her time, and if the curse was in play, it would have found a way regardless of whether she stepped on that plane. You see, you're *not the one who put the curse in motion. It simply used the plane as the most expedient method of killing her.*

That made me feel a little better, even though I felt guilty thinking so. "I guess you're right. If the curse was out to get her, it would kill her no matter what. Gods, I hate Gretchen and I've never even met her." I stood, finishing up my meal. It had all been delicious, but I felt oddly anxious. "Maybe I'll check out the desk Nonny sent me. I really haven't had a close look at it—I was planning on having her tell me about it."

That's a good idea. She sent it to you for a reason. I'm not sure why, but go look through it, anyway. And with that, Esmara vanished.

The desk was a rolltop, heavy, large, and made of oak. I stared at it, rather daunted. We had stuffed it in the library for the time being, and it filled a good share of the small room. With a sigh, I looked around. Killian was right. This was a beautiful house, but it was too small for us. He needed a home office, I needed a bigger office, and I still didn't like the fact that my ritual room was in a hidden compartment. Maybe we *should* move into his house and I could rent this one out.

Xi rubbed around my legs as I stared at the cramped room. "Hey, little one, what's up?" I asked, holding out my arms. She jumped into them, purring loudly.

Magic, she said. *The wood has magic in it.*

I blinked, glancing down at her. "Are you talking about the desk?"

The big wood thing. Magic. Lots of magic.

I gnawed on my lip, considering the desk. I hadn't even opened the drawers. Finally, I brought one of the standing lamps over to it and settled down in a chair. Then I began to open the drawers, one by one.

The first drawer was empty, but I wasn't done there. I'd watched enough mysteries and crime shows to do more than just glance inside it. No, I slid the drawer out, turning it over.

Wow, this is real wood, not just MDF or laminate. The bottom was solid. I slid it back in, then pulled out the middle drawer. Inside there was a small key, which I held up to the light. It was made for a small lock. I frowned, moving the light again to illuminate all of the cubbyholes and drawers. The top of the desk held a series of openings that reminded me of mail slots. The bottom of the desk had seven drawers, two smaller ones and one larger on each side, and the one in the middle. Each one had a keyhole on it.

As I began to open the drawers, starting in the upper right, I completely removed each drawer from the base, turning it over. I finished with the right-side drawers and was onto the center one, but when I tried to open it, it was locked.

"What have we here?" I muttered, fitting the key into the lock. It fit, but when I tried to turn it, the key resisted. The lock had rust in it, I figured. Pausing, I tried to remember where the WD-40 was. Then, I remembered that Killian had last used it in the garage so I dashed outside with the flashlight. It took me a few minutes, but I found the can on the lowest shelf over the workbench. Grabbing it, I ran back inside. I sprayed down the key and the lock the best that I could and, after another minute to give it time to work, I inserted the key again. This time, it still resisted but I managed to turn it.

When I slid the drawer open, I saw several things inside. There was a sheaf of papers, made of what looked like actual parchment, and then what looked like a gold necklace with emeralds. The moment I touched the papers, I caught a glimpse of a cow. The papers were actually vellum, and I gingerly fished them out, careful not to crumple them. They were so brittle I worried they might fall to pieces in my hands. As I set everything on the desk, it occurred to me that they hadn't seen the light of day since the time of my great-great-grandmother.

I sat back, contemplating the items I had found. I wanted to read the papers, but a glance at the clock told me that I should be getting ready for tonight's walk. I replaced everything in the drawer and locked it again, then attached the key to my keychain before heading out into the blustery night.

The rain had come in with a vengeance and the leaves were swirling off the trees en masse. By November, we wouldn't have any of them left to fall. Sometimes we had drier autumns, which led to the magnificent color change. But usually, it was wet like this—the leaves sodden brown and yellow on the ground instead of vibrant reds, bronzes, and coppers. I loved the autumns when the trees put on a show, but given we needed the rain after having a dry summer, I wasn't unhappy.

I had crossed the porch to the steps when I suddenly felt queasy, like something was wrong. Whirling, I expected to see someone lying in wait for me, but no one was there, and the porch light was bright enough to illuminate the entire space.

Frowning, I took a tentative step back toward the front door, but then stopped. I would be running late if I stopped to investigate, so I turned back around and hurried down the steps to my car. One feature I loved about it was that I could press a button on the key fob and it would turn on the interior lights, allowing me to see if anybody was inside. I glanced in the backseat, but all was clear, so I got in and, fastening my seatbelt, affixed my phone to the hands-free device.

As I started the ignition, I said, "Jerica, text Killian."

"What do you want to say to Killian?" responded the AI.

"Be careful when you come home. I thought there might be someone hiding on the front porch but I didn't see anybody. It was probably my imagination, but keep an eye out."

"Your text to Killian reads: BE CAREFUL WHEN YOU COME HOME. I THOUGHT THERE MIGHT BE SOMEONE HIDING ON THE FRONT PORCH BUT I DIDN'T SEE ANYBODY. IT WAS PROBABLY MY IMAGINATION, BUT KEEP AN EYE OUT. Do you want to send it now?"

"Send now."

"Your text has been sent." Jerica fell silent for a moment, then she said, "You have an incoming text from Killian. Should I read it?"

"Yes, please."

"Killian's text reads: I'LL BE CAREFUL. IT'S AN ODD NIGHT. WE'RE ALMOST DONE WITH THE SURGERIES. I DON'T KNOW HOW BUT WE MANAGED TO SAVE THE DOBERMAN'S LEG. THE ROTTY'S EYE WASN'T AS LUCKY. I'LL SEE YOU WHEN YOU GET HOME. TEXT ME WHEN TO EXPECT YOU. Do you want to reply?"

I thought for a moment, then said, "Text Killian."

"What do you want to say to Killian?"

"I love you. I'll see you later."

"Your text to Killian reads: I LOVE YOU. I'LL SEE YOU LATER. Do you want to send it now?"

"Yes, send."

"Your text has been sent." Jerica fell silent.

As the rain turned into a downpour, I turned the windshield wipers on full speed and the *whoosh-whoosh* was mesmerizing. I slowed even more. Hydroplaning on some of the streets around here could only lead to disaster. As I navigated to the office, I felt oddly insular. In the past few days

I'd gone from feeling normal to feeling isolated. By the time I reached the house in which we'd moved our offices into, I was almost panicking and I had no idea why. I jumped out of my car and stood in the freezing rain for a moment before heading inside toward the light and warmth.

Hank took one look at me and frowned. "Are you all right?"

I shrugged. "I don't know. I'm not sure what's going on but ever since my grandmother's death…no, actually, ever since that blasted funeral Killian and I went to on Friday night, I've felt out of sorts. I'm feeling overly anxious, it feels like I'm being watched, I'm feeling the pressure of my family curse—given that's what Esmara said was responsible for Nonny getting on that plane in the first place."

"Are you sure you're up to tonight?" Tad asked, leaning on a cane. He'd taken to using it after a long day, but it was a far cry from how weak he'd been after his liver surgery.

I thought about his question. Normally I'd blow everything off as just nerves, but I realized that something wasn't normal. Even if this was just me processing grief, I needed to pay attention to my needs. But I couldn't pinpoint anything that said "Don't go"…just a faint sense of ill ease.

"I should be fine. I don't know—maybe my planets are going through a rough phase or something. I don't spook easily. But at least I'll be hyper aware for the walk-through tonight. Let's go."

I helped Hank and Caitlin carry the equipment out to the van. Wren was at home with Walter, her husband. He'd been diagnosed with MS recently and the change in him was dramatic. Wren had money to hire a caregiver for a while, but the changes were taking their toll on her—she was tired a lot, and she didn't smile as much as she used to. An incredibly spiritual person, Wren had doubled down on preserving her peace of mind as much as possible.

"Let's get moving," Tad said. He locked up as we swung into the van, Hank behind the wheel.

My hazmat suit was still in there and I set the bag aside, grimacing as I thought of the astral worms. "You do realize we'll probably be called out on more argenium worms cases, given I think they have to have spread."

"They're ugly suckers, and they do taint energy and suck it up, but they're more of a pest than anything else. It's not like they're Mothman or...Bigfoot." Hank's voice dropped as he took the curve at a slow and cautious speed. I could tell he still felt guilty over everything that had happened because of his obsession with the creature. And truth was, I still dreaded facing the two bargains I had made in order to help us retrieve Tad. If I hadn't, he'd be dead and probably Hank as well. Bigfoot wasn't the big cuddly teddy bear so many people wanted him to be.

"Remind me about the Shoners—they're going to be there tonight, right? I don't have a good feeling about letting them in while we go through the house. I do sense there's something big and nasty in there." I chewed on the inside of my lip, tired of the uneasiness that I was feeling. It was getting old and I wanted to shrug it all off and go back to my cheery mood that I'd been in Friday, before the funeral. I felt guilty —neither Darby nor my grandmother had chosen to die—but the fact was their deaths seemed to have precipitated my plunging mood, and I resented it.

"They'll be there, but we can keep them out of the house if you like." Tad turned to me. "Seriously, you seem to be in a real funk. Are you sure you're up to this?"

I let out a long sigh. "I don't know if I am or not, but the spirit isn't going to stop haunting them, and they're in danger. That much I can tell you, and I don't intend to let something happen to them if I can help prevent it."

"Just don't try to go all Buffy over whatever's in there—

not without checking with the rest of us. We're just here to observe." Tad caught my gaze and held it.

"Sometimes I hate that you're so much younger than me and yet you can order me around, you know that?" I said, but I laughed. Tad was around twenty-six, compared to my forty-two.

He was well above genius level. He was also human, and he longed to be witchblood. But he *was* psychic—sometimes too much for his own good.

"Deal with it, Jaxson," he said with a laugh. "But…"

"I'll be cautious and I promise to try to avoid stirring things up. However, you realize that my very presence there —*our very presence*, with the FLIR and the EVP and other gadgets—that's not going to go unnoticed by whatever spirit's hanging out there? Whatever it is, it's going to be aware of what we're doing."

He snorted. "I know, I know. Just…you can be a little impulsive at times."

"Me? I'm not the one who…" I stopped.

I had been about to say that I wasn't the one who ran off to wake up Bigfoot, but I didn't want to hurt Hank even worse. He felt bad enough as it was. The fact was, though, his obsession had led to Tad nearly dying, and it had put me in a delicate position with two very powerful beings who had helped us out. And *I* was the one who would be paying the price for that. While I had forgiven Hank, there was no way I could forget. I had my back to the wall.

Hank cleared his throat. "Just say it. I know you were going to. And I don't dispute the facts. My obsession put everyone in danger, led to Tad's being seriously injured, and now because we needed the help, you're indebted to the Crow Man and the Fae. Hey, I'm willing and able to take your place on those promises, you know that. I'll bind myself to them in your place."

I stared at the floor. After a moment, I decided to meet the issue head-on.

"You're right. I *am* angry at you. Nothing could deter you from following Bigfoot, and you dragged us all along. Tad almost died. And even though you're willing to take my place in the line of fire, you know they won't go for that. Trust me, I checked into it. I looked up every source that I could find. If you offered yourself in place of me, they'd laugh. Or they'd trick you into joining me. The Crow Man, maybe not, but he's very specific and I rather doubt he'd let you take my spot. I'm angry but…I'll get over it. I just wish you would have thought first, but there's no shutting the barn door once the horse is out."

"She's right," Caitlin said. She'd been unusually quiet during the exchange. "You two—Hank and Tad—seem to have gone gung-ho, all-in on hunting Bigfoot without even stopping to think of the ramifications. I don't know what you expected to happen. Tad, you're more levelheaded than that and you still just gave in and made us all go out there. Without January, both of you would have died. You were *both* stupid and you know it!"

Tad pressed his lips together and stared at Caitlin. But then, he let out a sigh. "I should have put the reins on, since I'm the boss here. I just knew how much this meant to Hank—"

"Yeah, well if someone's blind but really wants to drive, you don't hand them the wheel, do you? Not unless it's a self-driving car!" Caitlin glowered. "I love you but damn, you can be an idiot."

Tad froze, then tilted his head. "What did you say?"

"I said you can be an idiot—"

But by now, I realized what he had heard and I broke out of my funk and into a full grin. "That's *not* what he means."

Hank laughed from the driver's seat. "I knew it!"

"What? What did I say?" Caitlin looked confused for a moment, but then the reality of what she had said spread across her face. "I… I…wasn't thinking—"

I realized at that moment that it had been the first time for those three words between them. "Don't take it back," I said softly.

Tad let out a long breath. "I…" He glanced at me, then exhaled. "I love you, too." Immediately, he realized he was still facing me and he blinked. "I mean—Caitlin—"

"I know what you meant, and so does she, goofball." I leaned back. "Why don't you try saying it to each other without anything else attached? Hank and I will mind our own business."

Caitlin started to sputter, but then she dropped the pretense. "I love you, Tad. I guess I always have—but I'm older than you—"

"Do you think that matters to me? I love you. I've been head over heels for a couple years but I… And once we started dating, I wasn't sure how or when or if I should say it." Tad broke out in a huge smile. "Well, that broke the tension."

"That it did," Hank called out over his shoulder. "I hate to put a damper on the convo, but we're almost at the Shoners'. By the way, I'll spend a lifetime trying to make it up to you guys. I let my obsession get in the way of reason. I can only say I'm sorry so many times, but I'll try to make certain you know I mean it. Now, let's get ready to rumble."

And with that, we parked, readied our equipment, and got ready to enter the Shoners' haunted house.

CHAPTER NINE

We headed up to the house. It was large—Craftsman in style, and it was weathered and worn. With a wide covered porch that spanned the front, the exterior was covered with siding that reminded me of snakeskin across the front and the upper stories.

In some ways, the house resembled an A-frame, with the second story smaller than the first, and the third smaller yet. Windows covered the front first floor, with a triple window in the center of the second story, and a small window in the center of the third. My guess was that the third story was the attic. The house, which was painted a pale cream, was weathered and the pillars holding up the overhang covering the porch were flaking paint. It definitely needed some work, though I suspected there were good bones beneath the worn exterior. The gabled roof was dark against the night sky.

I stood there for a few seconds, staring up at the window leading to what I suspected was the attic. There was a pale flickering light in the window as though someone was standing by it, holding a candle. I glanced around the yard. Two huge oak trees sat to one side, while a weeping willow sat on the other side of the lawn. Tall gates partitioned off the backyard from the front on both sides. As I looked around, looking for the Shoners, my attention kept being pulled toward the light in the attic. The rest of the house was dark.

A few moments later, Terry and Brenda pulled into the driveway. We had parked in front of the house. They got out of their car and joined us.

Brenda gasped. "The light up there—that's the attic. We turned off all the lights before we left. We didn't want any chance for a fire because of a shorted fuse or anything like that. So I made certain everything was off."

"Does anybody have access to your house except you? Does anybody else have a key?"

Terry shook his head. "No, we had the locks changed the day we moved in. We have the only keys. We were going to give one to our friends, but all this ghost business happened first."

"I want you to stay out here in your car. Are there any rooms in there you'd rather we don't go? Do you have any pets?" I asked.

Brenda shook her head. "If we had pets, they would have come with us. We'd like to pack a couple bags tonight while you're here—so we have a change of clothes to take with us when we go over to Vern and Melony's house tonight."

"We can do that. If that's what you want, then you should come in with us now, though. Our presence might stir up the spirits enough to where we'll have to get out fast by the end. Both of you, hang close and don't go wandering off by yourselves," I said. I turned to Caitlin and Hank. "Are you ready?"

They nodded. Tad was staying with the van to man the computers that the FLIR and EVP were connected to. They were wireless, though we'd occasionally found that wired worked better. We planned on setting up some surveillance cameras tonight, so we could get an idea of what we were facing. Paranormal activity didn't always present when we first went to examine a building, be it a house or a shop.

"Okay, then, let's go. Terry, Brenda—follow Caitlin. Hank will follow you. I'm going in first...I suppose I need the key?"

Terry handed me the key off his key ring. I slowly advanced on the house, hoping for an easy entrance. But on the way up the stairs, Caitlin was watching the EMF device.

"The activity's already spiking, even from out here. Be cautious when you open the door, January. Don't just barge in on this one."

I snickered. "I never *barge* in anywhere. Well, I guess I do, but I won't this time." I carefully inserted the key in the lock and turned it. The door creaked ever so slightly as I pushed it open. Instantly, I was assailed with the smell of something decaying. I pulled back onto the porch and turned around.

"Did you leave any food or anything out? Any meat?"

Brenda shook her head as Terry said, "No, I emptied the garbage before we left. There's some food in the fridge, but no meat or anything. We're vegetarians."

That didn't bode well.

"All right then. Be aware, something stinks to high heaven inside." As I once again opened the door and stepped inside, the odor was so strong it almost made me gag. I grimaced and looked around as I flipped on the light switch.

Light flooded the room, illuminating a tidy but jam-packed area. They obviously hadn't had time to fully unpack because, in addition to the furniture, several stacks of boxes filled what I suspected was designated as the dining room. An empty china hutch sat against one wall, the glass doors blown out. Shattered glass covered the floor and nearby table.

"Did that happen before you left?" I asked, pointing to the hutch.

"After," Brenda said, her voice almost squeaking. "My beautiful hutch..."

"Well, you can get new panes for it," Caitlin said.

"Okay, everybody in? Don't wander off alone. The energy here is so thick we could cut it with a knife." And in truth, it was thick—thick like sludge, with the smell to accompany it. I felt a pull from both the stairs and what I assumed was the kitchen. The stairs were to the back left, leading up before turning back on themselves.

There were two openings in the dining area, one of which was a door to the right of the dining room. The opening to the left was an archway. I suspected the archway led to the kitchen.

"What's behind that door? And does the archway lead to the kitchen?"

Terry cleared his throat. "The door leads to an office space. And yes, the arch leads into the kitchen. What do you think is in here?"

"Too soon to tell. I need to walk through the house, but to do so, I need you guys to hang back. Caitlin, start setting up a couple cameras in here and keep the Shoners company. Hank, come with me, please." Given the strength of the stench, I had no desire to take a jaunt through the house alone.

Hank and Caitlin made sure that the equipment was working, and then, bringing the EVP and one of the FLIRs, Hank followed me as I headed into the kitchen.

"You want them to get their clothes first?"

"Not quite yet." When we were through the archway leading to the kitchen, I turned to Hank and whispered, "Whatever is in here is big. I'm not sure it's safe to have them in here at all."

"I know," he whispered back. "But they have to have clothing and I don't think they're flush enough to just go buy new togs."

"We'll take them with us on the way upstairs," I said,

turning back to the kitchen. I gasped. "Are you getting this on camera?"

Every drawer was open, and silverware was levitating in the air. Knives, forks, spoons, all hovered around us, gently spinning. That included the kitchen knives as well as the butter knives, which meant we could easily find ourselves on the wrong end of a paring knife—or a cleaver.

"Cripes. Do you see the fog?" I asked.

A thick mist was rising, covering the floor as it rolled through the room.

"I wish we'd done research before coming," Hank said, filming the floating silverware.

"Me too. I had to decide to examine my great-great-grandma's desk instead of getting on the computer. I'm sorry." I had totally glossed over my priorities. "I really didn't think it was going to be this bad."

"Neither did I," he said. "I'm the one who usually does the deep dives on these cases. I'm sorry I didn't jump in to help. Now we're in deep without a paddle."

"I'd say without a lifejacket." I held my breath, waiting to see what would happen. Best case: the silverware would drop back into the drawers and stay there. Worst case: we'd be impaled by knives, cleavers, and forks. "Can we ease back out of here, do you think?"

"We can try. Go slow, don't bolt, and get ready to dodge."

"I don't fancy dodgeball with these kinds of balls," I muttered as I began to inch back toward the archway. The forks began turning toward us. "We need to be quick and jump to the sides," I said softly.

Hank reached the archway first, since he'd been behind me. "Get out of the way," he said to the others. "*Now.*"

As soon as he vanished through the archway, the forks began to rattle in the air. I took a deep breath and launched myself toward the arch as a hail of silverware came flying my way. I ducked as I cleared the doorframe, rolling to one side. At that moment, a hail of forks came streaking out of the kitchen and embedded themselves in the wall opposite. Luckily, they missed everyone.

Brenda shrieked. One of the forks began to quiver, trying to pull itself out of the wall.

"Caitlin, get them outside, now!" I shouted.

Caitlin dropped everything to rush the couple toward the door. As they moved, the fork yanked itself loose and began to whirl toward them, tines forward, whirling round like it was affixed to a drill bit. They managed to stumble outside seconds before it splintered into the door.

Hank and I slowly backed up, trying to steer clear of the broken glass from the hutch. He turned the FLIR toward me but I wasn't surprised to see the temperature around us plunging. I could see my breath in front of my mouth now.

At that moment, a loud crash from overhead echoed through the house as carnival music began to play. Crap, the circus had come to town but I didn't want on any of its rides.

"Ya think we should get out and go do some research?" I asked.

"If we don't, we're toast," Hank said.

None of the silverware was threatening to skewer us at the moment, so I decided to tune in and see what I could come up with. We were close enough to the door to make a run for it, should we need to. I took a deep breath and closed my eyes, trusting Hank to keep an eye on me.

As I went lower into trance, I began to feel the swirl of energies surrounding us. It was like a macabre symphony, rather than just one blaring cacophony. There were the lighter notes—at least two ghosts trapped here, both young and terrified. And beneath them, I sensed another spirit—this one felt motherly, as she tried to protect the children.

But below that, a deep and sonorous well of anger—so deep that it didn't even feel human.

Whatever was after the spirits rolled through—and then I saw it. An ancient serpent, coiled to strike. And the anger over being woken up reverberated off the walls. First, the spirits had woken it, and now, the Shoners had intruded. The house was filled with activity that spiraled off the serpent—and most of it was pure anger over being woken out of a long slumber.

I groaned as the serpent turned toward me. It rose up like a cobra, ten feet tall, almost to the ceiling, only instead of silvery skin the serpent had brilliant blue scales. It was so bright it was hard to look at, and drops of venom dropped off its fangs. Yet it was ethereal, beautiful in its danger.

"January, January! Wake up, we have to get out of here!" Hank shook me until I opened my eyes. I glanced around and found the entire room was bathed in a blue light, and I realized I was having trouble breathing.

"Go! Get out of here," I said, shoving him toward the door. He grabbed my hand and pulled me behind him. As we stumbled out onto the porch, he turned and slammed the door behind us and we raced down the sidewalk toward the car.

"What the fuck was that?" Caitlin shouted as we came racing toward her.

We turned, staring at the lights inside the house that cycled on and off as though they were on a timer gone mad. The light had taken on that same blue shade, and I backed away toward the car, not certain whether the snake could get out of there.

"I don't know," I told Caitlin. I turned to Terry and Brenda. "I'm sorry, but there's no way we can allow you to go inside. You wouldn't come out alive. I suggest you hit up a thrift store for a few outfits until we can clear this out."

I didn't want to say that I thought they should cut their losses and run. They couldn't just walk away, on the hook for a house they couldn't live in and that probably wouldn't sell easily unless they accepted some developer's lowball offer.

"What do you think we have in there?" Brenda asked.

"First, there are two children's spirits trapped there. I don't know who they are or from what time period, but they're definitely caught. There's another spirit—a woman—trying to protect them. And then...then there's whatever that serpent is. I think it might be off the dreamtime and I think somebody attracted its attention. Or, for some reason it was sleeping in the land and somebody woke it up. Whatever the case, the serpent's angry—it didn't want to be disturbed and now it's spewing out its wrath."

"Snake? Dreamtime? You aren't talking about an actual snake, right?" Terry asked.

"Right. Think more astral snake. Whatever the case, don't go back inside without contacting us first. I'll do some research tomorrow and we'll call you." I paused, adding, "I'm serious. If you walk in that door now, you might not walk out alive. And trust me, there are things worse than death. Like finding your spirit at the mercy of that snake."

"We promise," Brenda said. They slowly returned to their car, glancing over their shoulders. I detected tears in Brenda's voice, but she said nothing as they got in and drove away.

We waited until they were gone. "We left a couple cameras in there. Did you have time to hook them up, Caitlin?" I asked.

She nodded. "Yeah, so as long as nothing destroys them, we should be able to get readings. Do you want to head back to the office, or just go home? I should go into the office and set up my station so it records everything going on."

"I'll go with you," Tad said. "Hank, you and January can go home once we get to the office."

I grinned, not wanting to say anything. I knew that she'd be staying the night with him. They had a lot to talk about, given what had slipped out this evening.

"I'll probably do a little snooping on the net from home," I said.

"Me too." Hank slid into the driver's seat as we took our places in the van again. As we headed out, I wondered what we were going to do about our new hell house.

CHAPTER TEN

Killian was waiting up for me by the time I unlocked the front door. I glanced around the porch on my way in but saw nothing. As I entered the house and shut out the storm, he hurried to greet me, pulling me in for a kiss.

"You're shaking," he said. "What happened?"

"Bad, bad, scene. Think hell house." I slid out of my jacket and he took it, hanging it up for me. I was both soaked and tired. "I have no clue what entity we're facing, but I want to find out before going back. I'm pretty sure it could do some major damage to us."

"Why did you tell me to watch out when I came home?" he asked.

I just wanted to fall into bed. It had been a long, eventful day filled with creepy astral worms and terrifying ghost snakes and, overreaching all of it, the loss of my grandmother. I was in no mood to dissect everything that had happened. I kicked off my shoes by the sofa and tossed my handbag on the coffee table.

"Here's the thing," I said. "I've been having some bad

headaches the past few days, and not feeling well. Some astral hitchhiker got into my aura. It's gone now, but it might be responsible for the way I've been feeling. I don't know. My stress levels are sky high, and that doesn't help matters either. When I headed out to do the walk-through tonight, I thought something was on the porch. Maybe some*one*. But I couldn't see anybody. But it bothered me so I asked you to keep an eye out. I don't know what it was, if anything."

"Headaches? Maybe you should see the doctor," Killian said, a worried look on his face.

"I'll be okay. It's just... I guess Nonny's death hit me harder than I thought."

"All right, but... So, the day was really bad?"

"You have no idea. Our first case this morning was stomach churning, and then tonight it was like we took a page out of *The Amityville Horror*." I dropped on the sofa, leaning back to stare at the ceiling as I put my feet up. "I want to go to bed, but I'm too tired to haul myself up the stairs. Did you feed the cats?"

He nodded. "I fed them and played with them. And I found the Chinese food in the refrigerator, so I finished my dinner. I have an idea," he said. "Why don't you take a warm bath and then let me give you a back rub. No innuendos, no *nudge nudge wink wink*. Just a nice, long back rub."

"That sounds absolutely wonderful. You're a good man, Killian. I can't wait to marry you."

He motioned for me to stand up, and before I could protest, he swept me into his arms and carried me up the stairs. It always surprised me how strong shifters were. I was an ample woman and most men would probably have trouble carrying me around, but for Killian, it was like carrying the cats. That was one wonderful thing about shifters. They were so strong that it made me feel light as a feather.

Upstairs, he deposited me on the bed and headed into the

bathroom, where he began to draw a tub of warm water and poured a large dollop of vanilla-scented bath gel in it. Then he returned to the bedroom and seeing that I was struggling to undress, he waved my hands away and began to take my clothes off for me.

"You know I'm too tired for sex tonight," I said, ruefully.

"You know that I know that already. Just let me help you. I love doing things for you." He dashed back into the bathroom to turn off the tub, then returned to the bedroom where he finished undressing me. I stood, heading for the bathtub, but Killian picked me up once again and carried me into the bathroom where he gently deposited me into the warm water.

I leaned back, my head against the bath pillow, as I sank under the blissfully warm ripples. Killian sat on the shower bench, which he pulled over next to the bathtub.

As I leaned back in the tub, he found a music channel on his phone that played old Celtic music. The keening of the fiddle along with the steady rhythm of the bodhran lulled me into a mild trance. I was half asleep, half awake, sliding into that delicious place where my body hung heavy as my mind soared free.

We didn't talk, and the only sounds of the room were the soft ripples of the water around me and the music. I was about ready to fall asleep when the mood of the room shifted. I opened my eyes, suddenly aware that everything seemed on edge. I sat straight up, covering my breasts as I looked around.

"What's that?" Killian asked, looking startled.

"Then you feel it too?" I asked.

He nodded. "It feels like something just passed through." He jumped up, warily looking around. I could tell he had gone into alpha mode, and he was sniffing the air as though he could smell something.

Feeling vulnerable because I was naked and in the water, I scrambled out of the tub, fully awake now. My robe was hanging over one of the towel racks and I quickly shrugged into it, tying the belt snugly around my waist. I closed my eyes, trying to suss out where the energy was coming from, but it seemed everywhere, darting around the walls.

Xi came racing into the room, her eyes wide. *Make it go away. It's dangerous. You need to kick it out of the house.*

"I know, Xi. We can feel it."

Before I could say another word, Xi suddenly flew into the air and was headed toward the tub of water. I caught her mid-flight, hugging her to me as she meowed pitifully.

"Get your filthy hands off my cat," I shouted.

Killian let out a loud growl, and was tearing his clothes off. I could see that he was changing, unable to keep the transformation from happening. Holding Xi to my chest, I hurried out of the bathroom, trying not to slip on the wet floor. In the bedroom, I yelled out for Esmara.

"Esmara! We need your help." My voice echoed through the room, even as something skittered across the walls in the bedroom, racing around all of them to complete a circle.

Killian bounded out of the bathroom, a beautiful gray wolf, his eyes gleaming as he took his place in front of me. Klaus was on the bed and he jumped into my arms along with Xi, both cats clinging to me as I held them tight. A loud laughter echoed through the room, ricocheting off the walls as it rebounded back and forth like a pinball.

Esmara appeared. Her eyes narrowed as she looked around the room. She held up her arms, hands to the sky, and in a voice that reverberated deeper than I thought possible, shouted, *Begone! Foul creature, leave now or I will destroy you.*

No sooner had she spoken that my phone rang. I glanced at it to see Rowan's name on the caller ID. "Rowan," I said, pressing the phone to my ear. "Please come over! It's an emergency. Please hurry."

"I'm on my way." My grandmother was succinct, hanging up immediately after answering.

Killian gently grabbed the hem of my robe in his teeth and tugged me toward the door. Still holding the cats, I followed him, slamming the door behind me, trapping the unwelcome visitor behind the door. I quickly made my way to the stairs.

On the main floor, Killian, still in wolf form, guarded me as I hurried to the living room. Wishing I kept the carriers closer, I rushed into the library where they were, sliding the cats inside them and shutting the doors firmly. They were safer there than they would be out. Still in my robe, I picked the carriers up and raced to the living room where I grabbed up my bag and keys and hotfooted it out onto the front porch.

The wind was still shaking the trees, and the gusts echoed loudly in the night sky. I cautiously hurried across the porch, my feet freezing on the slippery rain-soaked wood. The temperature was falling for the night, and I shivered as I hustled through the wet grass toward the driveway.

Once by the cars, I unlocked the door of Killian's SUV and placed the cat carriers in the back, shutting it firmly after I did so. Opening the driver's door, I slid in and unlocked the passenger side, stretching as far as I could to open the door.

Killian bounded in, tongue hanging out as he panted. I reached around him to shut the door again, then sat there, staring at the dashboard. I wasn't sure what to do. Should we get out of here? But Rowan was on the way, and if anybody could handle wayward magic, she could.

In the end, I just turned on the overhead light and then turned on the ignition so I could heat up the car. I was freezing, the flimsy robe barely covering anything. As I stared up at my house, I wondered what the hell was in my house and what did it want? All I knew was that, whatever it was, it had threatened Xi, and *that* would not go unpunished. Nobody but nobody touched my fur babies and got away with it.

Ten minutes later, Rowan and Tarvish appeared in the driveway, in Tarvish's new truck. As they slid out of the vehicle, I leaned back, relieved. My grandmother was here and she would make everything okay.

"What the hell is going on?" Rowan asked as she settled into the backseat next to the cat carrier containing Xi. Tarvish managed to get into the other side, although he had to set Klaus's carrier on his lap.

"I have no idea," I said. "So much has been going on the past few days and I have no clue what to think about most of it. I need your help. *We* need your help."

At that moment Killian, sitting on the front seat, changed back into his human form, fully naked and gorgeous. Rowan, who had been leaning between the front seats, let out a chortle.

"Congratulations, granddaughter." She put just enough spice in her words that Killian blushed and looked around for something to cover his penis. Rowan handed him her straw hat and he groaned, but placed it over his groin. "So what happened?"

"I don't know where to begin. But tonight, something showed up in the bathroom causing havoc and it tried to drown Xi. My kitties aren't safe in my own home and I don't know what to do." I felt horribly guilty, as though I had opened the door to a predator.

My grandmother got out of the car. She motioned to me. "You, come with me. Tarvish and Killian, stay with the cats."

She was carrying a bag over her shoulder and I could only chance a guess at what was in it. Rowan never came unprepared.

I followed her, still nerve-racked by what had happened. But I felt safer with Rowan than I did with just about anybody. We dashed up the front stairs and she didn't even hesitate. She just walked over to the front door and slammed it open, charging in. I followed more slowly.

Once inside, she took a quick look around, frowning. "Okay, I can tell that something was here, but it's gone now. Whatever it is, though, it's chaotic and powerful. You said that you were upstairs when it showed up?"

I nodded. "Yeah, we were in the bathroom. I was taking a bath and it almost killed Xi. I want it gone. Nobody attacks my cats and lives to tell the tale."

"Come on, let's take a look." Rowan jogged up the stairs and I followed her. My stomach clenched, but she pushed open the door and peeked in. "Oh good gods. I assume that you didn't do this." She stepped inside, moving out of the way so I could enter behind her.

The bathroom was a mess. Ectoplasm oozed off of almost every surface. The water that had been in the bathtub was gone—the plug had been pulled. And across the mirror, streaks of what looked like snotty blood dripped down the glass.

"Is that blood?" I asked.

Rowan leaned toward it and sniffed. "No, just colored ectoplasm."

She glanced at the vanity, which was covered with a jumble of items. "Start from the beginning."

I told her about the argenium worms, and then the Shoners' house. "When I got home, everything was okay. Then...this."

"I suspect that you did pick up a hitchhiker and that it's

been coming and going freely through the house." Rowan looked around, frowning. "I feel there's some sort of revenge going on. But it doesn't involve you, not exactly."

"Then what the hell is happening?" I frowned, trying to think through all the possibilities. "What about the funeral we went to the other day? Could I have brought it home then? Killian's friend Darby was jealous of him. And then, the case Conjure Ink is dealing with—could I have brought home something hanging out with the Shoners?"

"Tell me about the walk-through tonight."

"Well, there was some sort of spirit—I'm guessing it's an ancient entity because it takes the form of a massive blue serpent. I believe that it's keeping several spirits trapped in the house. I'm not sure if it's demonic or just astral in origin. But that doesn't seem like it would lower itself to this sort of crap." I pointed toward the ectoplasm. "I don't know how or where this came from, but I don't appreciate some ghost sneezing gallons of snot all over my bathroom."

Rowan stifled a laugh. "That's a good way of putting it. This is going to be hell to clean up. I know, I've dealt with it before. I'll stay and help you. For now, let me take a quick walk through the rest of the house. If I'm right and whatever it is, is gone, I can help you set up a barrier to keep it out. I *can* tell you one thing: whatever sort of spirit this is, it isn't as powerful as I am."

Relieved, I followed Rowan out into the hallway and we checked over the rest of the house, including my ritual room. The place was clean. The only spirit around was Esmara and she was as pissed off as I was. Once we knew the place was free of ghosts, Rowan set in with her incense, dagger, and protection water and warded every corner of the house. Tarvish and Killian brought the cats back in, and the four of us cleaned the bathroom.

As she had predicted, the ectoplasm was a mess to clean

up. Surprisingly, the best method of cutting through the slime was dishwashing liquid. Another hour and we had everything cleaned and put away again. We met down in the living room, and Killian brought out a bag of potato chips and some dip, along with several sodas. As we settled down to talk, Xi and Klaus cuddled up on either side of me. I kept them close, thinking how terrified I had been when Xi's life was threatened. I had to do something, and do it quick. I couldn't ever let them be in danger again.

CHAPTER ELEVEN

Killian and Tarvish listened while Rowan and I discussed what had happened. Esmara lingered in the corner, quietly observing. I was fretting because I had planned to do some research on the Shoners' house, but being attacked in my own home seemed more urgent so I texted Tad and asked if he and Caitlin could research the lot themselves. I told him what had happened and he texted back for me not to worry and said they would get right to work.

"Rowan thinks I picked up a hitchhiker," I told Killian and Tarvish. "I doubt if it was at the walk-through tonight, because odd things have been happening for a couple days now."

"The only answer is that you picked up some tag-along at the funeral, then." Killian scooped up a chip full of dip. "I know it seems far-fetched, but could it be Darby? He and I weren't exactly friends at the end, remember. Could his spirit be terrorizing you to get back at me?"

I thought about it for a moment. It was possible. After all, one of the better ways to force someone to do what you wanted them to was to threaten their loved ones. It seemed to follow that hurting your enemy's loved ones would be worse torture than just hurting them.

"How badly do you think Darby wanted revenge?" I asked.

Killian thought about it for a moment. "We hadn't seen each other for a long time. I suppose his resentment could have grown during all that time. Maybe finding out that I'm happy and engaged to a woman who is the love of my life pushed him over the edge. Maybe it was like a slap in the face, given he was dead." He buried his face in his hands.

"You may be right about that," Rowan said. "Do you know what his mental condition was before he died?"

"Not good," Killian said. "He was addicted to drugs and booze. Do you think he followed us back from the funeral?"

I cautiously nodded. "I'm beginning to think that's exactly what happened. It might account for Richie's behavior at the wake."

Killian shook his head. "No, that was *all* Richie. Trust me. But you *have* been feeling watched in the past few days—that could be Darby."

"If it is, then it won't be difficult to dislodge him." I grimaced. "But there's a bigger concern in all of this—the fact that my aura's open enough that something can latch onto me. Also, my house wards obviously failed. Why isn't my magic working the way it should be? I'm not the strongest of witches, but I'm not the weakest, either." I turned to Rowan. "Could it be because of that damned curse?"

Xi let out a *purp* as she stretched and yawned, then settled back into a ball of fluff and went back to sleep. I absently stroked her back and she purred.

Rowan glanced over toward the corner where Esmara was standing. "Ask your great-aunt."

I turned to Esmara. "*Could* this be happening because of

the curse?" Then, remembering the desk, I added, "I found something when I examined Nonny's desk this evening. I found an emerald necklace and some parchment in a locked drawer. I didn't have time to read it—"

A necklace? You found Ellen's emerald necklace? Esmara looked almost frantic.

I nodded. "Apparently so. Why?"

She was wearing that necklace when she died, if it's the one that I'm thinking about. She had it on when Delcartan the artist painted her portrait. Two days after he finished, she fell off a cliff, into the sea below. The rocks below were jagged, but even if they hadn't dashed her to bits, she would surely have drowned. She left her daughter Colleen motherless. Colleen's father remarried later, but Colleen and her stepmother never truly got along. They didn't hate each other, but both were relieved when Colleen and Brian decided to emigrate to the United States.

I thought about that bit of news and told everyone what Esmara was saying. "So, somebody hid Ellen's necklace in the desk? Why didn't Colleen inherit it?"

That I don't know, except my mother once told us that her father thought that the necklace played a role in her mother's death. He gave Colleen a bigger dowry, since he thought the necklace—which was worth a great deal of money—was dangerous, and he refused to tell her where it was. Esmara frowned, shaking her head.

So, Ellen's husband had probably hidden the necklace to keep his daughter safe. "Do *you* think that the necklace is cursed?"

Esmara thought for a moment, then said, *No, I don't. Ellen was cursed, not her jewelry. But her husband wouldn't have known that. If he had, my guess is that Gretchen Wyre would have been strung up and left for dead unless she removed the curse, and even then Ellen's husband would have probably killed her. They didn't mess around back then.*

"Now, the million-dollar question. Do you think the curse

is affecting my wards?" I really didn't want to die like my grandmother. And I absolutely didn't want to die thanks to a ghost.

Esmara considered my question. After a moment, she said, *Yes. I think it's possible. The curse can make magic fade. It didn't for Naomi, but it did for me, before I died. I only regained my magic after my death. Which is why you* have *to find Gretchen and ask her to remove it.*

"What happens if she won't? Or can't?" I really didn't want my thoughts to run along this direction, but that seemed to be their destination.

"We might be able to approach the Crown Magika. There might be something some of their upper-echelon witches can do. Especially given the fact that I know where the bodies are buried. And that's *not* hyperbole," Rowan added. "I wonder why Teran didn't take care of this when she was younger? Or her mother? Or her sisters? Ask Esmara why your family let it go on unchecked?"

I turned to Esmara. "You heard her. What's the answer?"

Esmara glared at Rowan and I was rather glad Rowan couldn't see the look. The last thing I wanted was the two going at each other. But after a moment, she let out a sigh and said, *It was a lot harder to locate people before the internet, and before phones. We didn't have the resources you do now. That alone made it difficult to find anybody, and Gretchen Wyre certainly wasn't standing there with a big sign saying, "Here I am!" We didn't have connections with the Court Magika, either, like Rowan. And trust me, we tried to remove it ourselves. My sisters and I cast a number of hex-breaking spells, but nothing ever worked.*

"How could you tell they didn't work?" It occurred to me that it would be difficult to tell.

There's a glow to our auras—you will get used to seeing it once you start looking at Teran's aura compared to other people's. It's a faint squiggly line, sea green, that blends in, but if you watch for a while, you can see it. You should practice. Esmara smiled sadly. *I'm sorry to say, the line's in your aura too. I can see it clearly.*

I looked down at my hands. I could see auras when I tried, but I never made a deliberate practice of it. "So, nobody else has this line in their aura?"

Not this one. Just the women of our family. You won't see it in the nimbus we spirits give off—now that we're dead, the curse is broken for us. But as long as it continues in the auras of our women, it means the curse is still active and will strike.

"And it's not in the men's auras?"

No, but if they have daughters, it will pass to them. And I can't be sure, but I fear that this hex may get worse as time goes along.

After a moment, I nodded. "Rowan and I are going down Thursday." I glanced over my shoulder. "Right? We're still on?"

Rowan, who was watching, nodded. "Yeah, we're going. We're not calling ahead, either, because we're not giving her any chance of running." She paused. "Was Esmara asking you about Gretchen?"

"Not exactly, but it all ties in together." I returned to the others. "There's a chance my magic is fading because of the curse." I sank down on the sofa, realizing just how serious this was. "I can't let that happen. I don't want to die too young because of a curse. I don't want to see my magic fade."

Killian was about to pull me into his embrace when Rowan shook her head. "No, this is no time for a pity party. We'll go down Thursday—and I picked that day for a reason. Astrologically, it's a good day to confront boundaries and limitations. And we need all the help that we can get."

I stared at the floor, a thousand thoughts running through my head. "I used to be so angry at my mother for ignoring my magical side. I wonder if she thought maybe it would allow me to live longer. She had to know about the curse."

"Oh, I'm sure she did," Rowan said. "And in her fear, she

might have thought she was protecting you by not teaching you about your lineage. Maybe she thought it would nullify the curse if she did so."

I hadn't thought of it that way. Maybe my mother had been trying to help me. "Well, whatever the case, we have to solve this. I don't know if I can go on, every time I turn a corner, wondering whether something's going to jump out and kill me because of some curse."

"We'll do our best," Rowan said. "Meanwhile, trust me. If Killian's friend is out to get you on a spiritual level, he won't be able to get back in here. Not through my wards."

I turned to Killian. There wasn't much he could say, so I just rested in his arms while Tarvish played with the cats.

THE NEXT MORNING I WENT TO WORK SUBDUED. I WAS hoping nobody else would notice my mood, but Hank picked up on it right away.

"Are you all right?" He asked.

"Honestly, no. I have a situation going on—"

Tad and Caitlin were close enough to hear and they turned around. So I figured I might as well tell everybody about what was happening. I called Wren over from her desk and we all gathered around the break room table. I told them about the curse and what we had learned about it, and I told them about the possibility that Darby's spirit was following me. Finally, I told them that my magic might be fading.

"Damn, that's harsh," Tad said.

"Isn't there anything you can do in the meantime? Until you actually get to go see Gretchen?"

I shrugged. "I don't know. It all seems so unbelievably formidable. I feel like I'm suddenly a million miles away from where I was, even a few months ago. I only learned about the curse a few months back, but even then I didn't quite comprehend just how far-reaching it can be. And it didn't occur to me that the Ladies died because of it. They all died far younger than they should have."

Hank was sitting at his desk, rubbing his chin as he listened. "You know, my family is connected with several well-placed witches. Let me make a few calls and see if I can find anybody who might know something about breaking hexes."

"Do you really think that if Rowan can't break it, somebody else might be able to? Rowan's the strongest witch I know."

Hank grinned. "Rowan's a firecracker, and yes, she's incredibly strong, but she's not necessarily the strongest witch around. Not by any means. It can't hurt to try, can it?"

I let out a long breath, but inside I was dancing a jig. If Hank had a friend who could figure out a cure for this curse, I would owe him so much. I could only hope that somehow, I wouldn't face the same fate as my grandmother and her sisters.

"Okay, thank you so much. I guess we'd better get to work for now." As preoccupied with my own future as I was, the fact remained that we had work to do, and whatever was haunting the Shoners' house wasn't going to sit around waiting for me to solve my own problems.

"What did you find out about the history of the house?" I asked, turning to Caitlin.

"There's a whole can of worms in that answer," Tad said. Caitlin nodded as she and Tad brought out their tablets. Tad motioned to her. "Why don't you go ahead and start?"

Caitlin sent us each a file of notes that she had prepared. As we opened them up on our own tablets, I stared at the picture of the house that was staring back at me. It was grainy, taken a long time ago, from when Moonshadow Bay had still been a relatively new community.

"It seems that the house used to be a boardinghouse. That's not uncommon, given how the area was being settled during that time. The house goes back to 1910. It was one of the first structures built here in Moonshadow Bay." Caitlin sorted through an actual file folder she had with her and pulled out a couple photographs. They definitely showed the house in its heyday. A hanging sign on the porch read Wilcox Boardinghouse.

"So it's over one hundred and ten years old," Hank said.

"Yes, and everything seemed on the up and up. At least superficially," Caitlin added. "It was owned by a woman named Analia Wilcox, a widow. I researched her background. She was a gun-toting, fiery-tempered woman whose husband died young. She had married a man over from Germany, whose name was William Wilcox. They had been married for only five years when he fell down a flight of stairs and died." She air quoted the word "fell." "After he died, Analia sold their house and, with the proceeds, bought the boardinghouse in 1915. The original owners had decided to move back to New York."

"Let me guess," Wren said. "There are questions about his death that were never answered."

"Oh, they were more than questions. There was a lot of speculation on how he came to fall down the stairs. Analia—Annie—said he was drunk, but nobody ever smelled liquor on his breath. William was a teetotaler. The doctor, however, made no dispute of her claim and listed his death as an accident on his death certificate. Interestingly enough, the doctor later bought the Wilcox house from Analia." Caitlin frowned, shaking her head. "Anyway, Tad did some research into the area on which the house was built."

"Yes. Unfortunately, the area on which the boardinghouse was built was originally the site of an outpost when Moonshadow Bay was first being surveyed for habitation. The outpost contained a post office and a general store, as well as habitation for three of the men scouting the area. It's unclear what exactly happened, but one night one of the men went crazy and burned the outpost to the ground, killing both himself and the other two men who lived there. Since the town had not yet been established, it took at least two weeks for someone to discover the remains of the fire. Luckily, it hadn't spread. This happened during the winter, so there was enough snow to keep the fire from catching hold in the nearby woods."

"So we have an outpost that was burned to the ground by one of the men living there, then the house was built and promptly bought by a woman who is suspected of being, at the very least, complicit in her husband's death?" I asked.

"It gets better," Caitlin said. I thought I detected a look of glee in her eyes. "Before the outpost was built, the area was used by one of the local tribes to hold their sick and infirm. It was basically used to sequester patients with communicable diseases. Smallpox was rampant, and although records are not clear because we don't have access, it's thought that at least forty-five members of the local tribes died from the disease in that area."

So we could place at least forty-five smallpox patients who died, an outpost that had been torched by one of the men living there resulting in several deaths, a potential murderess, and who knows what else on that land. That definitely made for the beginnings of a first-class haunting.

"What about native lore? Were there any spirits that were supposed to have inhabited that area? We know about the land wight from when I first came to work here at Conjure Ink, and that creature isn't all that far away from here. We also have the Mystic Woods, which surrounds not only the town, but the entire area."

"Native legend has it that some creature came out of the

Mystic Wood into the area. They called it a massive serpent, as thick around as a man's waist, with wings. You know, it reminds me of an Asian dragon, at least by description," Tad said.

"So we're dealing with a *dragon*?" I said, groaning. "That would explain the blue snake that I kept seeing. But why would it be keeping the ghosts in the house? It doesn't seem to feed off of them, or does it? Or is it a ghost dragon? And what would a ghost dragon feed off of?" I knew I was being ridiculous. We had encountered Bigfoot. We encountered Mothman. We had encountered all sorts of critters from other planes and dimensions, but facing a dragon? That was something I had never expected.

"I don't know if it's an actual dragon, or something else. The fact is, you *saw* it, but did you see a *spirit*? Or an actual creature peeking into our dimension?" Hank asked.

"We did some more research regarding dragon and serpent lore," Caitlin said. "What we discovered is that there was another sort of creature whose name is synonymous with dragon, and is often used interchangeably. We're talking about wyrms. Now when you follow the roots of that word back, you *do* run into a connection with dragons. But what if wyrms are separate, apart from dragons? What if they've never been the same creature, but are, instead, related? Remember Quetzalcoatl? He was an Aztec god, a feathered serpent. Perhaps a dragon of sorts. Suppose he was the god of an entire race? Or the *father* of the race? Or the avatar of one of the beings from whatever species they are?"

"What exactly was Quetzalcoatl a god of?" I asked. I was familiar with the name, but not so much the individual.

"Let me look it up," Tad said. Moment later, he began reading off from a website.

> Quetzalcoatl was also known as Kukulcán by the Mayans. At first he was considered a vegetation God, connected with the earth and water. But during the Toltec culture, they turned him into the God of the morning and evening star. He became a god of death and rebirth, and somehow during that time he became connected with a plumed serpent.

"I don't think we're going to find any concrete answers, given how many conflicting legends there are. But suppose there is a race of plumed serpents on the astral plane and one of them somehow got itself trapped in that house? Maybe it just wants out? Maybe it can't get free," Hank said.

"How would we know if it's trapped?" I asked.

"I suppose we could try to ask it. If it came from the Mystic Wood, maybe something lured it out? What do we know about Analia Wilcox? Was she witchblood?" Wren asked.

"I looked into her heritage, and she was actually from a particularly powerful family of witchblood, but they were at odds with the Court Magika and were ousted early on. I wouldn't place her as belonging to the Covenant of Chaos, but she was definitely a chaotic sorceress." Tad let out a sigh. "Here's the kicker. She fell down the stairs at the boardinghouse and broke her neck. Just like her late husband fell down the stairs at their old house. There were a couple of witnesses at the boardinghouse, and one of them said it looked like she was pushed. As she fell, she screamed out William's name—in fact, they quoted her as saying, 'Curse you William, curse you to hell.' So it makes me wonder if William's spirit didn't do her in?"

"Well, if he did, is *he* still in the house today? If he is, then did he follow her there and somehow get trapped? Or did he decide to hang around," I said. "One thing we can be sure of: there's been plenty of psychic activity in that house throughout the decades. Are there any reports from people who lived there after she died?"

Caitlin nodded. "The house passed through over *fifteen* different owners. The shortest length of time anyone spent there was three weeks. The longest—six years. There is also a private cemetery out back. I doubt that Brenda and Terry knew about it."

"Who's buried there?" I asked.

"I'm not sure. But I think we should go out there and take a look. There's a lot going on there, and it's not going to stop on its own." I glanced around the table. "Well, shall we head over there and see what's happening? Then I need to go back to the Yoga Now studio and complete the second part of the ritual to rid it of the argenium worms. Next thing you know, we'll be fighting a giant earthworm," I said, shuddering.

Laughing, the others readied themselves for the trip.

CHAPTER TWELVE

When we arrived at the house, Brenda and Terry weren't there, but we hadn't expected them to be. I still had the key that Brenda had given me the night before, so we could get in if we needed to. But before we went back *into* the hell house, we decided to take a look around out back. The house was on at least half an acre, and the yard extended back to the Mystic Wood. As I stared at the section of the woodland, I shivered. There were so many nuances to the energy of the forest, and here it felt dark and wild.

The yard was overgrown, although part of it had been mowed, and the lawnmower sat in the middle of the backyard, drenched by the rain. I wondered if it was toast, but you never knew. Outside yard tools were often very resilient, but it was riding mower and I had no clue about their motors or how they ran.

At the back of the lot, there was a black chain-link fence dividing the yard from the Mystic Wood. I hadn't seen it at first; the chain-link blended in so well with the vegetation that pressed up against it. To the left, the yard was thick with weeds, the grass and vines almost waist high. I tried to catch a glimpse of what was beyond the fence to the left, but several large cedars blocked my line of sight. If there was a house on the lot next door, I wasn't seeing it. A small fence enclosed that corner of the yard. Again, black chain-link.

"Tell me you're Gothic without telling me you're Gothic," I said.

Hank gave me a confused look. "What?"

"Never mind," I said. "Over there, I'm positive that's where the graveyard is."

As we crossed the lawn, I could feel we were being watched from inside the house. I turned to stare at the old Craftsman, gazing at the second-story windows that overlooked the backyard. I froze.

From one of the windows, I could see sparkling white eyes glaring down at me. I poked Hank and nodded toward the second floor. He looked and gasped, stepping back.

"We aren't alone," I said.

"Well, you're right about that," he said. "We have a number of onlookers, I think."

I glanced over at the door. There was a faint light seeping out around the edges. It suddenly occurred to me that if the ghosts could sense the energy in my aura that marked me as cursed, maybe that was why they came at me so much. I felt incredibly vulnerable, knowing what I knew now, and the thought made me want to run and hide. Forcing myself to turn away, I steeled myself and headed over to what I assumed was the graveyard.

The chain-link fence ran approximately fifty feet long and twenty feet wide. There couldn't be *that* many people buried there, although if you planted the coffins several inches apart, you could probably get close to thirty or so, if you didn't leave much room between them.

As we entered the cordoned-off area, I noticed that the

vegetation was different. The grass was waist high, yes, and ivy vines had crept in, winding around most of the fence posts. To the far right outside of the fence, a huge old yew tree overshadowed the graveyard, its twisted trunks weaving together in a chaotic pattern. It reminded me of a snake ball, where the snakes all intertwined, one big orgy of writhing bodies.

I noticed that a row of shrubs lined the fence. I wasn't the best at identifying vegetation, but I immediately recognized it as deadly nightshade—belladonna.

"Yew and belladonna, the perfect graveyard plants. I wonder if someone who owned this place used them for spell work. Belladonna growing over a gravesite is going to be far more potent magically than belladonna just growing in an herb garden."

Inside the fence, poking out from beneath the waist-high grasses, were several headstones. A number of them had broken and toppled over, but there were at least two rows of graves, and I estimated there were at least nine graves in each row.

Caitlin knelt by the nearest grave marker, which was flat on the ground, hidden in the grass. She pulled back the weeds to look at the headstone. "This has the name 'Arbuckle Trotsky' on it. Nineteen-twenty to nineteen-seventy. There's nothing else written, no epitaph or anything else."

I joined her, then moved to the grave next to Arbuckle's. As I brushed back the weeds I saw another inscription on another headstone.

"This one belongs to someone who was named Renée Trotsky. Nineteen twenty-two to nineteen-ninety." I looked around. "How were they still burying people out here in 1990? Wasn't that against the law by then?"

Caitlin was busy looking up information on her phone. "Interesting," she said. "In 1962, a Henry Caudell owned the house. He applied for a permit from the city to turn his backyard into a graveyard. Moonshadow Bay granted his request. So, legally, the backyard is still considered a cemetery. Ten months later, Henry left and the house and land went into foreclosure."

"So when you buy the house, you buy the graveyard."

"Right. Another couple, Jake and Irene Fitch, had already contacted the bank, trying to figure out who to talk to about buying the house. The bank sold to them, primarily because they offered to pay the back taxes and full price on the house. They moved in on January 3, 1963. They moved out May 14, 1963, and the house set empty for another five years. Finally, they sold it to a woman named Mary Skelley in mid-1968. Mary Skelley lived here for twelve years until she died in 1980."

"And all that time, they were still burying people here?" I wondered just how hard up some people had been to own a house.

"Apparently," Caitlin said. "So far, I haven't found any names on the graves that match the names of people who actually owned the house. I can't find anything about Jake and Irene Fitch, the couple who lived here in 1963. Or at least, I'd need better databases than just searching on my phone. I suppose we should come up with the names of everyone who has ever owned an interest in this place, and see if we can match any to the names of the dead here."

"Well, we know what happened to Mary Skelley. I wonder if she's buried out here."

Hank and Caitlin began to check the names of each of the graves. We were right, there were eighteen in all. And sure enough, Mary Skelley had been buried in her own graveyard.

"We're not going to find out all the answers this afternoon. What else do we need to see?" Tad asked, gingerly stepping into the graveyard behind us.

"Wait, what's that?" I asked, pointing to the back of the graveyard. There, hidden by the grass, was another gate leading into the neighbor's yard. We couldn't see very far through the thicket of trees that surrounded us. I made my way through the grass and headstones to the gate. It was rusted shut, but it was obvious that the path continued on the other side. I wondered if there were any more graves over there, so I asked Hank to come help me.

He began to fidget with the gate, jiggling it for all he was worth and finally, the latch opened and the gate popped ajar. He stood back, nodding to me.

"Do you want to go first?" he asked.

I wasn't sure if I wanted to or not, but it had been my idea, so I decided to step up to the plate. "Of course."

Hank swung in after me and we ventured into the yard next door. The entire site looked feral, all the foliage and shrubs gone wild. I strained for a glimpse of the house but I couldn't see anything. The trees were thick, almost as though we were in the Mystic Wood itself.

I turned to Hank. "Is this a residential lot?"

Hank shrugged, pulling out his phone. He held it up to his face and said, "Hey, Jerica? Who owns 4875 Wild Berry Street in Moonshadow Bay?"

Jerica responded, "The owner of 4875 Wild Berry Street is the Moonshadow Bay Arboretum Society, who purchased the property in 1995."

"Tell me, who runs the Moonshadow Bay Arboretum Society?"

"Monica Whisperwind became the president of the Moonshadow Bay Arboretum Society in 2019. She took the position following the disappearance of the former president, Romy Stropes, who vanished on a trip to Mount Rainier National Park."

Hank pocketed his phone. "So, do you think the

belladonna was first planted over here, and then spread to the Shoners' house? Or do you think it was planted in the graveyard and then spread to this lot? And by the way, given the Arboretum Society still owns this land, why have they let it go to hell?" He looked around. "Look at this—you can tell there were herb gardens and flower gardens here, but everything looks overgrown. I know it's autumn, but really?"

"Yeah, I see what you mean. Let's take a look around." Catching sight of a fairly straight wooden stick, I picked it up. Deadly nightshade was as dangerous as it sounded, and there were other plants that could be far more toxic, by touch as well as ingestion. Given the Arboretum Society had plenty of witchblood members, I didn't want to chance picking up somebody's deadly little plant child.

As we began to wander around the lot, I used the stick to push back the bushes, checking beneath them. I wasn't sure what I was looking for, but I had the feeling I'd know when I found it.

Then I paused. There was a pile of sodden leaves in one corner, beneath a massive oak tree. The trunk of the tree had to be five feet in diameter, and about half the leaves were still clinging to the boughs overhead, though they were yellow and wet. The next big windstorm would bring them down.

I began to scrape the leaves beneath the tree aside. Noticing what I was doing, Hank put on gloves, crawled beneath the tree, and began shoving handfuls of leaves out of the way. After a moment, he stopped. Beneath the leaves, there was a round wooden circle, about two feet wide, lodged into the ground. There was no handle on the circle, and the wood was weathered, having lost any paint it might have once had on it.

"What do we have here?" I tapped the wood with the stick and the resulting *thunk* sounded hollow. "That's covering up some sort of hole."

Hank tried to pry it up but he couldn't get his fingers around the sides. "It's wedged in tight. I need a crowbar. I think there's one in the van."

"I'll get it," Caitlin said, who had caught up to us. As she ran off, Tad cautiously joined us. He was still using a cane, but he was getting more stable on his feet every day.

Hank watched him as he picked his way through the vegetation. The look on his face said everything. I knew he felt bad about Tad, and I knew he would have given anything to go back in time and change the outcome of our ill-advised camping trip.

"Here, do you need help?" Hank said, jumping up. "There are a lot of rocks in the undergrowth."

"No, I'm going slow. I'll be fine," Tad said. Just as he spoke, he toppled over. "Damn it," he said, sitting up and slamming his cane on the ground. "I thought I..."

Hank took a deep breath. I could tell that he was uncertain whether or not to offer him help. He glanced over at me. I crossed to Tad and silently offered my hand. He stared at me for a moment, then took it, leaning on me as he stood up. The surgery had taken a lot out of him, and Tad wasn't a strong man to begin with.

As he stood, I quickly bent and brought up his cane. I handed it to him, then turned back to Hank, not asking whether Tad was all right. If he had hurt himself, he'd say something.

"Here," Caitlin said, racing back through the gate, crowbar in hand. She tossed it to Hank, who caught it. She must have sensed the tension because she glanced over at Tad, frowning. "What..."

"Nothing," Tad said. "I just turned my ankle on a rock. I'm all right."

Caitlin nodded, then moved over to my side. Tad joined Hank, keeping enough distance in case something came flying out of the hole, while Hank grunted, prying at the lid. As he worked, Caitlin leaned close to me.

"What happened?" she whispered.

"Tad fell and Hank was about to pick him up without asking if he needed help. I stepped in and diffused the situation, but I'd walk softly for a bit."

Caitlin lowered her voice. "At some point Tad needs to confront Hank. Tad blames himself for everything that went on, and he feels horrible about you having to make promises to the Fae and to the Crow Man. But let's face it, Hank pushed hard on the issue and Tad likes to make us happy. He wanted Hank to have a chance to fulfill his dreams. But I have a feeling that at some point there's going to be a breaking point and Tad's going to actually face his anger over what happened. He's been repressing it since it happened. I don't know what the outcome will be. I hope it doesn't end their friendship."

I shook my head. "After this long? Those two are like brothers. This whole mess may strain things, but they'll stay friends."

"I hope so."

At that moment, Hank let out another huge grunt and flipped the wooden circle out of the hole. It landed on the ground, exposing a dark hole beneath. I stiffened, watching to see if anything was coming out—we'd had our share of monsters hiding in holes, and I no longer took anything for granted.

After a moment, when nothing popped out, I moved forward. The tiff between Hank and Tad seemed to have been forgotten as we knelt on the ground and cautiously peeked over the edge.

Hank pulled out a high-beam LED flashlight and turned it on, shining it down in the hole. I had imagined a deep well, scary deep so we would have to take a chance if we wanted to find out what was down there, but the hole only went about ten feet down. The sides of the hole were compacted dirt, and I paused as the light hit something sparkling. I lay down on my stomach, craning my neck to see as much as I could, as I directed Hank to direct the light toward the sides. There, we could see crystal spikes pointing out of the sides of the hole, all over. Crystals had been embedded into the dirt, all over the sides. This was no natural hole.

"Oh man, look!" Caitlin pointed toward the bottom.

Hank directed the light down to the bottom, and there we saw a kneeling figure. The figure's hands were tied behind its back, and from what we could tell, the body was actually skeletonized, bones gleaming.

"The hands are tied together," I said, a shiver running up my spine. "And if I'm not wrong, doesn't the skeleton look child-sized?"

I knew I was right. That wasn't an adult down there. It was a child. I glanced up at the house, of which the top story was visible from behind the garden gate. "We better call the police. No child tied their own hands behind their back and then somehow got in a kneeling position in that hole and trapped themselves. I think we're dealing with murder."

Tad sat back, an ashen look on his face. "Call them. This is beyond our authority."

I put in a call to Millie.

Millie Tuptin was a German shepherd shifter, and she was the chief of police. We had gone to high school together. Millie was the best person I could think of to hold her office. She was practical, and she fully accepted the nature of magic, even though she was a canine shifter. Dog and wolf shifters were leery of magic in general. Killian and his family were rare amongst their kind in that not only did they not fear magic, but they didn't mind being associated with witchblood. Millie didn't care for it, but she had made a point to understand magic because it helped her on the job.

"Hey Millie, we have a situation. We're over at 4875 Wild Berry Street. We are investigating a haunted house case next door, and we happened to make our way over into the lot owned by the Moonshadow Bay Arboretum Society. We found a covered hole in the ground, and when we pried the cover off, it looks like there's a child's skeleton down there, with its hands tied behind its back. We haven't touched it or disturbed anything, not since we opened it up."

There was silence on the other end of the line, then a low sigh. "I'll be there in ten minutes. I'm actually in your neighborhood right now. I'll put in a call to the medical examiner, and we'll bring everything we need. Don't touch anything that you haven't already touched, and don't let anything go down that hole until we get there."

As I hung up, I turned to the others and told them what she had said. "I suppose we're benched until they get here. Tad, why don't you and Caitlin wait here while Hank and I go examine the graveyard. She didn't say anything about us not continuing our investigation, and that seems like the next thing to do. We need to take down all of those names on the markers."

"All right. Go ahead." Tad sounded tired, but I had the feeling it was more depression over the argument with Hank.

As Hank and I returned to the graveyard garden, I kept my eyes open for anything else unusual. Once we were back in the enclosed cemetery, I turned to Hank. I knew Tad couldn't hear me from here.

"You *do* realize that Tad is going to explode at some point? He's holding a lot in, and you know exactly what. I'm not going to beat a dead horse. We all know that the trip for Bigfoot was a bad idea, but we all know that we had a choice.

We could have spoken out more, we could have said no. But Tad is such a good guy, and he never wants to play bad cop."

Hank raised his hand, stopping me. "I know, I know. I'll have a talk with him later today. We'll hash it out, I promise. Now, let's get busy and take down all these names so we can look them up in comfort. I don't like that house," he said, staring up at the Shoners' house. "It gives me the creeps."

As Hank read out the names, I wrote them down, verifying the spelling as well as the dates. Most of the names were unfamiliar. I kept thinking about the body in the hole. There was something about a child's grave that always made me sad. The promise that was never fulfilled, the hopes and dreams that never even had a chance to form. It was like an unfinished symphony; you'd never find out just how complex or beautiful it could have been.

All of a sudden, Hank looked up. I followed his gaze and saw the medical examiner and her team, heading toward Tad and Caitlin. We waited for a moment, then went back to identifying the graves. There were two that didn't have markers on them, and I wondered if we could get away with digging them up to find out if there was anybody down there. But even as I was thinking about that, Hank stopped. He was reading the names of the last two graves in the second row.

"What is it? You look like you've seen a ghost. I know we're in spirit central right now, but..."

Hank gave me a solemn shake of the head. "No jokes. This is serious. The last two graves here? One belongs to Allie Turner, and the other to Saratoga Joe." When I made no response—primarily because neither name rang a bell for me—he continued. "Saratoga Joe is from Louisiana. He was a biker who vanished from town about fifteen years ago. I knew him, but I always steered clear because he was a prime member of the Covenant of Chaos. And Allie Turner? She was a local girl who disappeared. I can't believe her grave's been sitting here all this time and nobody ever knew. They searched for her, but found no sign. Could she have been buried here all this time? It's been twenty years since she vanished. Can you go get Millie and bring her here? I'm pretty sure Allie's still a missing-persons case."

I stared at him, my mind racing. Not only had we discovered the body of a child in a well—or what I had thought was a well—but now we had uncovered the grave of two missing people? What the hell was going on? And why had everything remained hidden for so many years? As I made my way over to Millie, my thoughts were racing a hundred miles an hour. I just didn't know *where* they were headed.

CHAPTER THIRTEEN

The minute that Hank showed Millie the headstone for Allie Turner, the cops went into high gear. She radioed back to the station for more officers, and not only did they cordon off the Arboretum's lot, but also the Shoners' house. As they began taking pictures of the headstone and the graveyard before excavating, I backed up toward the house. Another group was over by the hole, examining everything around it before bringing up the child's skeleton.

"Well, we sure stirred up a hornets' nest," Caitlin said, joining me. Tad was right behind her, and Hank had gone back to the van to find some food. This had turned into far more of an expedition than we had expected.

"I know. I'm supposed to be down at the yoga studio within the hour to perform the second part of the ritual. I don't think I'm going to make it." I pulled out my phone, debating on what to do.

"Do you have your equipment with you for the ritual?" Tad asked.

I shook my head. "No, I left it back at the office. I'd have to go back to the office first and then downtown. I wonder what happens if I let it go beyond twenty-four hours before performing the second part of the ritual. I'm going to call Lisette and ask her."

It had suddenly become very noisy with all the cops around. I walked away from them, mostly to get a little quiet. Lisette answered on the third ring.

"Why, January, what can I do for you?" She sounded busy, so I didn't beat around the bush.

"I'm not going to be able to get to the second part of the ritual for the yoga studio for at least another couple hours. Does it have to be twenty-four hours exactly?" I didn't bother explaining why. The why didn't matter.

She paused. "No, but don't let it go more than another six hours. Otherwise, you'll have to start again because the worms will start the cycle again. I think you have enough ingredients in case you have to begin all over again."

"Yeah, I do. I hope it won't come to that. We've got a serious situation going on, in terms of the ghostly arena." I didn't tell her what we had just found. I wasn't sure if Millie would want the information out there.

"I hope nothing too dangerous?" Lisette asked.

"Unfortunately, there's a lot of danger involved. I'm really getting tired of maniacal ghosts and astral creepy crawlies. But it seems to be my fate to deal with them."

"Well, dear, at least you are suited for your work. And no, I'm not calling you a creep. You just have the ability to handle these things, so better you tackle them than someone who isn't trained." She hesitated, then added, "Is there anything else I can help you with? I'm sorry, but I have a reading coming in and I need to prepare."

Grimacing, I hastened to say, "I'm sorry. I'll let you go. You answered my question and I thank you."

As I hung up, I turned back to watch the commotion in the graveyard garden. A shiver ran up my spine again, and I looked overhead. I wasn't sure what I expected to see, but as I stared overhead, the dark clouds began to rumble and a flash of lightning split the sky, the neon blue illuminating the gray clouds surrounding it.

The lightning seemed to jump from cloud to cloud and then—as I watched—a blazing bolt forked down, striking the top of a fir tree in the lot next door. Startled, I let out a shriek and hit the ground. Caitlin joined me, and both Tad and Hank threw themselves over the top of us.

Every hair on my arm was standing up, and I was out of breath from the pile on. Very slowly, Hank crawled backward, then he stood and helped Tad to his feet. The two of them reached down for Caitlin and me. Tad grasped Caitlin's hand as Hank took mine and helped me stand up. I dusted myself off, feeling winded.

"That was too close for comfort," Caitlin started to say, but I shook my head and pointed at the top of the tree.

"Fire!" I looked around for Millie.

The top of the fir had caught on fire, and although we had been soaked by drenching rains, the lightning had been hot enough and strong enough to set it ablaze. The flame was speeding down the narrow top of the tree, toward some of the barren branches below. Even though the fir was an evergreen, there were parts of it that were dead and devoid of live needles and those branches would go up like kindling.

Hank set off running for Millie, calling out, "Call the fire department! One of the trees got hit by lightning and it's on fire!"

Millie turned, her gaze instinctively traveling up the tree. "Oh, mother fucking son of a bitch, just what we need!" She pulled her phone out and punched a number, bringing it to her ear. A moment later she was talking in a loud voice. "Send over a couple of fire trucks to 4875 Wild Berry Street. We have a tree on fire due to a lightning strike. It's burning brightly, and there's plenty of other vegetation, plus an old house here." As soon as she pocketed her phone again, she turned back to the crews examining the graves. "Keep working until we have to leave. The fire department should be here within five minutes—there's a station nearby."

She turned to us. "Stay out of the way. Don't enter the Shoner house unless I give you permission. We don't know what's going to happen with that fire right now. Make sure your vehicles are out of the way so the fire truck can make it in."

Hank ran out front to make sure our van wasn't blocking the driveway, while Caitlin, Tad, and I all tried to find a place out of the way where we could still watch. It was pouring by now, hailstones raining around us like pebbles falling from the sky. They were pea size, but they still stung when they hit bare skin. I frantically looked around for some protection from the hail and led Tad and Caitlin over to beneath an apple tree that was in the backyard, far away from the burning fir. The hail was still falling, but at least we had some protection from it.

"Well, I can think of better ways to spend an afternoon," I said. I glanced up at the house and groaned. I pointed toward one of the upper windows. "Look!"

Lights in the upper floor were flashing off and on, and I could see some sort of vapor filtering out from the closed windows. It wasn't actual smoke, or at least I hoped it wasn't, but it had to be some sort of etheric mist, or something like that.

"Oh wonderful, *everybody's* getting in on the act," Tad said.

At that moment Hank came running back, carrying a couple of umbrellas. He handed one to Tad, who shared it with Caitlin, and then opened the other and held it over my head. He scooted in close but I didn't object. For one thing, I liked Hank and I wasn't at all uncomfortable around him.

And two, anything to protect us from the hail right now. I would have crawled into a sleeping bag naked with him, if it would mean the stinging ice pellets would stop hitting us.

"Is the hail putting out the fire?" I asked glancing up at the tree.

Unfortunately, the treetop was fully engulfed. It would have taken a deluge to snuff out the flames. There was just too much dry wood up there.

The sound of sirens echoed from the street, and within another couple minutes the firemen raced in, dragging the hose over their shoulders. They looked up at the tree and I thought I heard one of them curse under his breath. One ran back toward the front and a moment later, the gate on the left side of the house crashed down as the firetruck drove across the grass.

Two of the men climbed in the bucket, bracing the heavy hose over their shoulders as the driver began to raise the bucket. As they did their best to aim the hose up toward the fire, I realized my head was beginning to hurt. Within seconds, it went from a mild throb to a splitting headache. It was so bad that I could barely think. I groaned, crouching down on one knee. As I held my head in my hands, Caitlin leaned toward me.

"Are you all right?"

I shook my head. "No, I don't think so. My head hurts—it's really bad."

I winced, going down fully on my knees. Caitlin began to rub my back slowly, trying to help. But all I wanted was silence and a dark room away from all the activity.

"I think I'm going to be sick," I stuttered out, my stomach churning. I tried to turn away as Caitlin smoothed my hair back from my face. I leaned forward in the grass and vomited, although not much came out except for stomach acid. Apparently, I had already digested my breakfast. Once again, Hank made a run for the van as Tad hurried over.

"January? January? What's going on?"

I shook my head, sweeping my hand across my forehead as I tried to fight off the waves of nausea. "I just... I just feel..."

Caitlin shoved a tissue in my hand and I wiped my mouth, then turned away and lowered my head to the ground so that it was resting on my hands. The cool pungent smell of the soil stirred my senses, and it was the only thing that smelled good. I could hear the firefighters shouting about the tree, and I could hear the clamor of the police officers over in the graveyard, but I couldn't sort out what was what. Everything was becoming a giant blur.

"We need to get her home," Caitlin said, her voice filtering in and out of my consciousness.

I mumbled something, but I couldn't even hear what *I* was saying. The next thing I knew, Hank had me up in his arms, and I protested that I was too heavy for him to carry but he ignored me, striding over to the van. It hurt to open my eyes, but when I did, I was lying on the floor of the van and Caitlin was squatting next to me. The van was moving, and the motion made me queasy again, but this time I didn't throw up. I needed to call Killian, I thought. I had to call Killian, but when I tried to reach for my phone I couldn't find it.

"Killian. I need to call him—" I tried to say, but Tad hushed me.

"Caitlin's already doing that. She has your phone. Just close your eyes and rest."

I wanted to protest. Part of me wanted to insist that I was all right, and part of me wanted to ask them to make sure that I was cremated because I felt like I was about to die. But instead of doing any of those things, I just let myself fall into the swirl of throbbing pain, and gave myself over to the cacophony in my head.

When I opened my eyes, I was lying down, and there was a cat by my side. The curtains had been closed in my room and the lights were off, but it was light enough to see. Caitlin was sitting at the bottom of my bed, a worried look on her face. Dimly, I could see Hank and Tad sitting in the corner. I squinted, my head still pounding. I still felt queasy, though I couldn't tell whether it was because I hadn't eaten or because of the headache.

At that moment, Dr. Fairsight came into the room. I was surprised to see her, since I didn't know she made house calls. I started to sit up, intending to get out of bed to say hello to her, but the room began to spin and I quickly lay back down.

"I'd stay on your back if I were you, or on your side if you prefer. Here, put this on." She handed Caitlin what looked like a sleep mask. As Caitlin slid it over my forehead, it felt cool, which was a blessed relief. I pulled it down over my eyes, grateful for the darkness and the chilling relief.

"Am I okay?" I asked. "I mean, I know I'm not, but I don't remember what happened."

"Your vitals are good. You don't have a fever. From everything I can see, you're physically fine except that you seem to have developed a migraine of epic proportions. You're going to be in bed until tomorrow at least. You need to get something on your stomach, but it should be light. Some buttered toast, and maybe some milk or something soothing." The next thing I heard was her say was, "Caitlin? Perhaps you could run down to the kitchen and fix her something?"

"I'll be right back," Caitlin said. She was standing next to Tad.

As I heard her move off toward the door, I realized I didn't like being in the dark. I started to push the mask up, grimacing as the faint light hit me. Even what little there was aggravated the headache.

"I don't get migraines," I said.

"Well, apparently, now you do. If I were you, I pull that mask back down because it's going to help." She sat down on the bed next to me. "When did it start?"

I pulled the mask back over my eyes and leaned back. "I'm not exactly sure. We were in the yard of the house we're investigating, and the next thing I knew, I felt queasy and my head started to pound. Then, all hell broke loose. I remember the lightning strike in the tree, and I remember the police digging up the grave—" I paused, trying to remember anything else but it was all kind of a blur. "I'm not sure what else happened after that."

"After that, you threw up and then fainted. Hank carried you to the van and we brought you home. Caitlin called the doctor on the way, and then she called Killian. He'll be here soon," Tad said.

"You didn't worry him too much?" The last thing I needed was for him to burst in all bent out of shape and worry about me. I couldn't handle much more excitement, whether it was worry, joy, or anything else.

"He doesn't think you're dying, if that's what you're asking," Tad said.

"There's something else I wanted to ask you," Dr. Fairsight said. Linda Fairsight specialized in treating Otherkin, including witchblood. We had worked with her a number of times before, and she had been the doctor on Tad's case. "I've noted something odd in your aura. I never noticed it before because I never had the opportunity to examine you, but there is a strange energy running through it—"

"I know what that is," I said. "At least I think I do. My family's under a curse, and my great-aunt, one of my spiritual guardians, told me that every woman in our family has a certain energy running through her aura. It vanishes when we die, apparently. But the fact that you saw it verifies that it's there and that I'm definitely under this curse. My grandmother Rowan and I are headed down to talk to the witch who cast the curse. We're going to Seattle on Thursday. I'll be okay by then, won't I?" I was suddenly very worried that I wouldn't be able to go with Rowan, and I would have to put it off yet again.

"I think you should be. You have tomorrow to rest up. And trust me, you *should* rest. The day after a migraine like this is never pleasant, and you'll probably feel somewhat hung over."

"Should she be working?" Tad asked. I started to protest but the doctor talked over me.

"I don't recommend it right now."

"I'm perfectly fine, or I will be—" I started to say.

"You had a major upset this week already, with your grandmother Nonny. I can't imagine how you can work under that stress," Hank said.

"What upset?" the doctor asked.

I let out a sigh. Somehow I didn't think I was getting out of this the way I hoped. "My grandma Nonny died in a plane crash a few days back. She was on the way to see me. That plane that the United Freedom Liberation Front brought down? She was on it."

As I said the words, everything crashed and I suddenly burst into tears. My shoulders shook and I tried to sit up so I didn't choke on the phlegm. I couldn't stop, and my entire body felt like it was shaking.

The next moment, Hank was beside me. I could smell his cologne. He wrapped his arms around me and I rested my head on his shoulder, the tears racing down my face from beneath the mask.

"How could they kill everyone aboard that plane? And the damn curse, it's to blame for her getting on that plane. We know it. Esmara told me." I yanked off the mask, then leaned forward, clutching my stomach as the tears continued to fall.

Dr. Fairsight leaned forward and took my hand. "No wonder you had this migraine. The stress may not be the only precipitator, but it certainly contributed to it. Tomorrow, I want to draw some blood and give you a more detailed examination. There's a chance that something else might be causing the headache—it could be a hormonal imbalance. But you should *not* be working right now, especially on stressful cases that tax your magic."

Caitlin returned at that moment, carrying a tray with a glass of milk on it, along with a dessert plate holding two pieces of buttered toast. She had also added a bowl of fruit salad. She set the tray on my vanity, looking at me with a worried expression in her face.

"Is everything okay?" she asked.

"I think it will be," the doctor said. "But January, I'm *not* clearing you to return to work until next week. You need to take a few days off."

"But the haunted house—the Shoners need me." I couldn't just let them down like that. "And the yoga studio—"

"Lisette can take care of the yoga studio," Tad said. "As far as the Shoners' house goes, it can wait until next week. They have a place to stay right now. The doctor's right. You need to rest and I'm not about to let you come back to work until Monday."

I was about to protest again when Killian came racing into the room. He glanced around, a frantic look on his face.

"January! Are you all right? What happened?" As he hurried over, Hank moved out of the way so Killian could take his place. Killian kicked off his shoes, then crawled on the bed next to me, shrugging out of his jacket. He looked over at the doctor. "What happened?"

"January has a bad migraine, and I'm taking her off work until next week. She needs to rest. Although I *am* giving you permission to get out of bed and go shopping or whatever else you might want to do. I just wouldn't drive, if I were you. I want you to relax. You need to take the time to mourn your grandmother, and to rest and recuperate. Whatever that energy is in your aura—the one you think is a curse—it has to be eliminated. It's causing havoc with you and your system. You say you've been dealing with spirits and a haunted house?"

I nodded, wincing as my head began to throb again. "Yes, it's part of my job. The past few days we've been dealing with some very powerful spirits and trying to get a read on how to handle them."

"No more of that, not until you're feeling better. Back off any activities like that." The doctor stood, turning to Killian. "She doesn't have to stay in bed, but she should be careful. I worry about vertigo striking, and we don't want her falling downstairs. Is there a bedroom on the first floor?"

Killian shook his head. "Not here, but there is over at my place next door. We'll go over there and stay there for the time being. What about driving? You said no?"

"Not until she feels better. You say you'll be next door? I'll drop in tomorrow around ten to see how you're feeling, January. Meanwhile, maybe heat up some broth and drink that, and go to bed and rest. Rest is the best thing for you at this moment. And if you're being troubled by ghosts, you'd better set up some strong wards against them. I don't think you're capable of fighting anything off right now."

I winced, feeling inept. "I just think this is a lot of trouble over nothing."

"Let me do the thinking right now. In fact, whatever that energy in your aura is, I'm positive that it's interfering with your magic. That alone can cause a migraine for someone who's witchblood. I'll see you tomorrow morning. Call me if anything happens tonight."

She handed Killian her card and closed her bag, heading for the door. As she exited the room, she paused and turned back. "Watch her. I've dealt with her enough to know that she's not one to take orders easily." With a smile, she waved and headed for the stairs.

I dropped my head back against the headboard, and Caitlin brought me over my toast and milk. As she settled the tray across my lap, I stared at it, thinking how complicated my life had suddenly become. I hated being limited. I hated having restrictions put on me. But as I looked up at Killian, I knew that there was no way he'd let me get away with fighting them. For better or for worse, I was off work until next week.

Resigning myself to the fact, I picked up a piece of toast and took a small bite of it.

CHAPTER FOURTEEN

After the doctor left, Caitlin excused herself. "I'm going to clean up your kitchen. I'll also make you some broth so that Killian can stay up here with you."

Hank looked around. "What can I do to help? If you're going to stay over at Killian's tonight, do you want me to crate up the kitties?"

I nodded. The cats liked Hank. I looked down at Xi. "Hank is going to put you in your carriers. We're going over to the other home—to Killian's home."

Xi looked up at me, her eyes wide. *You don't feel good. You worried me. When they brought you home, you didn't hear me.*

"I know, sweetie. I have a very bad headache. It's called a migraine. We're going to need to sleep over at Killian's house. So please tell your brother to go with you and Hank, and to let Hank put you in your carriers. You won't be in there long."

Xi stretched, then leisurely jumped off the bed and went looking for Klaus. Hank followed her, winking at me. Sometimes he liked to call me Dr. Dolittle, and he always seemed to get a kick out of the times I would talk to Xi in front of him.

Tad stretched, wincing. "Make sure she doesn't come into the office. If she does, we'll drive her straight home. Do not worry about Brenda and Terry Shoner. We'll make sure they're okay, and we'll tell them that we can't do anything until next week. Meanwhile, Caitlin, Hank, and I will do some more research and talk to Millie about what we found out in the garden. I'm not sure if the body in the hole has anything to do with the Shoners' house, but we'll figure it out eventually." He leaned on his cane, limping slightly as he headed for the door. "Damn this leg. I know my liver took the brunt of it, but somehow my leg didn't come out quite so peachy."

As he left the room, Killian turned to me and reached out, brushing my hair out of my face. "I was so worried when they called me. I knew it was too soon for you to go back to work."

"The doctor said the curse is affecting my magic, and I think that might be causing part of the headache. I know stress is part of it, too. I'm scared," I admitted, finally facing my fear. "What if this curse does something to me? What if it affects my brain or something?"

"On Thursday, you and Rowan will go down and talk to Gretchen. It will work out. It has to work out. We have to keep hope and we have to be optimistic. And if for some reason Gretchen refuses—well, there are ways to make people comply." His eyes darkened, and he seemed to grow taller.

I caught my breath, staring at him. Killian was growing into an alpha wolf. He had never been a beta in his Pack, but he hadn't been an alpha either. He'd followed more of the lone wolf path. But the longer I was with him, the more he seemed to be evolving.

Thank gods, he wasn't an alpha in the macho, hyper testosterone way that I hated in men. But he was becoming what was known as a *noble alpha*, someone that his Pack would look up to. Killian's Pack was more advanced than other wolf packs. They were more progressive, especially regarding strong women and alternative lifestyles.

"I'm not sure what you mean by that," I said. "And I'm not sure I want to know."

"Don't worry about it," he said. "Tarvish and I had a long talk the other day, and we agreed that there are many ways to convince people to do what you want them to do. For now, tell me what clothes you want me to pack. You just stay in bed until we're ready to go."

As I told him what to pack, Caitlin returned, carrying another tray with some chicken noodle soup on it. She set it across my lap and handed me the spoon.

"Eat every bite while I'm here. Hank has the kitties crated, and I put together a bag of their food. We'll carry everything over for you. We just need the keys."

I teared up, feeling weak and all too vulnerable. I slowly began to eat. "You guys are so sweet. Thank you so much. Give Hank a hug for me, would you? You know, I could do some research at home on—"

"Oh, no," Caitlin said, cutting me off. "You won't be doing any work whatsoever. Killian, you might want to take away her computer."

"Oh, hell no. I need that! I'd go crazy without it. I promise, I won't do any work. I'll watch YouTube videos, and movies. Just don't take away my tech." I held up my hand. "I promise, on my oath as a witch."

"You saw her swear," Caitlin said, laughing as she turned to Killian. "Give me that suitcase and I'll carry it downstairs. I think January's going to need your help because even if she says she's capable of walking down the stairs, I'm going to guarantee you that she's not. I've had migraines in the past and the vertigo is absolute hell."

"What about the dishes—" I started to say, but Caitlin waved away my protests.

"I did them." She picked up the suitcase as though it weighed ounces instead of pounds, and darted down the stairs. Sometimes I forgot that she was a shifter, and she had that same exceptional strength.

As Killian gathered me up in his arms, I let out a long sigh. But I said nothing as he carried me down the stairs, and then sat me down on a chair near the front door. Caitlin dashed back up the stairs again, returning with all of the used dishes. She carried them into the kitchen and I heard her rinse them and put them in the dishwasher. Finally, we heard the hum of the dishwasher and she returned.

"My purse. I need my purse and my keys."

Caitlin retrieved them as we headed through the living room toward the front door. She made sure the sliding glass doors were locked and then followed us out, locking the front door behind her.

Hank was waiting for us over at Killian's as Killian helped me through the front door. I sat down in one of the recliners in the living room as Killian thanked Caitlin and Hank, taking my suitcase and purse from them.

Hank handed Killian back his keys. "I put the cats in the guestroom—I took a stab at it, since it's the only bedroom I found on the main floor. I set up their litter box and put food and water out for them. We'll call tomorrow and see how you're doing, January. You take it easy."

As Caitlin and Hank took off, Killian locked the front door behind them. Then he helped me into the guest bedroom, and settled me in the king-size bed. As I stretched back, he turned on a nightlight in the bathroom and then turned off the main light. The blessed darkness eased my eyes, and I realized how incredibly tired I was.

"I'm exhausted, and I had no idea just how exhausted I was. I feel like I could sleep for a week."

Xi and Klaus bounced up on the bed, curling up at my feet. I closed my eyes and realized that I felt incredibly protected in Killian's house. He didn't use magic, so I wasn't exactly sure what made me feel so safe, but I was grateful for it.

"I'm going to get a bite to eat, and then I'll come in and join you. Sleep if you can. I'll bring some water for you when I return. Your suitcase is over on the ottoman, and your purse is on the dresser. We can unpack tomorrow when you wake up. I'm calling in first thing in the morning and taking the day off. Mike can handle the cases we've got."

He leaned down and kissed me gently on the forehead. "I hope you know just how much I love you," he said. "I think about you all through the day when I'm at work. I think about what we're going to do together in the evening, I think about your body and how much I love to touch you, to kiss you, to fuck you. You invade my thoughts constantly, January. I wouldn't want to live without you. Please be careful. You're the only treasure I need."

"I love you too," I whispered, too tired to be poetic. "You're everything I ever wanted in a mate. Hurry back."

As much as I wanted to stay awake until he returned, the blessed darkness of the room beckoned, and I felt safe and cushioned. With Xi and Klaus keeping guard at my feet, I allowed my eyes to close and fell into a deep sleep, thankfully free of dreams until the morning.

I WOKE UP AT TEN AM THE NEXT MORNING, HEADACHE-FREE but still feeling exhausted. It felt like every ounce of energy had been sucked out of me. I sat up in bed, looking around the room. Killian had a nicer house than mine—it was bigger and more modern. It definitely felt like a man's house, with dark wood trim and furniture, and buttery cream-colored walls. I tried to assess how I felt, but it was difficult. I was in that foggy stage where I had slept too long, but the migraine had left its mark. My body felt beaten up, even though I hadn't done anything to hurt myself. A moment later, the door opened quietly and Killian peeked in.

"Oh good, you're awake. Dr. Fairsight is here to check you over."

I nodded, yawning before I said, "Bring her in. I just woke up."

Dr. Fairsight entered the room, glancing around. "Nice house," she said. "So, how are you feeling today?"

One thing I liked about her was that she never used the royal *we*, and she never patronized her patients. Even when I didn't understand something, she patiently explained what I needed to know, without acting like she was superior or I was stupid. There were a lot of doctors out there who treated their patients like cash cows and refused to listen to their concerns. So I valued Dr. Fairsight for her bedside manner as well as for her expertise.

"I feel like I have a hangover. I slept all night, at least I think I did. I don't remember waking up." I glanced over at Killian. "Did I get up last night at any time?"

He shook his head. "No, I don't recall you getting up. If you did, I was asleep." He glanced over at the doctor. "I'll leave you two alone. Call me if you need me." He shut the door behind him as he slipped away.

I pushed myself to the edge of the bed, swinging my legs over. "I don't know if I've ever had a migraine before in my life," I said. "Why should I start now? Is it the curse, do you think?"

"Your aura's definitely off. That could contribute to the

migraine, but I honestly don't think it's the cause. I have a suspicion, given your background, but I want to know more before I say anything. So I'm going to work up a series of tests. While you're not middle-aged for someone who's witchblood, the fact is that anyone at any time can have their health shift. Your hormones could be out of whack. You could be developing a stress reaction to your work. There are a lot of things that could be happening."

I glanced up at her, afraid to ask what I was thinking. "What about a brain tumor?"

"What makes you ask that?" She set her bag on the bed and pulled out her stethoscope.

"Probably watching too many medical shows? I don't know. It's just... Migraines are headaches, and headaches aren't something I usually encounter." I took off my nightgown and wrapped the bed sheet around me so she could check my heart. She then checked my blood pressure, and took a look in my eyes.

"Blood pressure is fine. In fact, it's a little on the low side. Your heart's racing more than it should be, but that could be white coat syndrome. Or it could be anxiety. Hold out your arm. I'm going to take some blood." I grimaced, glancing away as she stuck my inner elbow with the needle and withdrew the blood. "At least you don't have rolling veins. I have the hardest time with a few of my patients—I can barely get blood out of them any way I try." After taking several tubes' worth and labeling them, she tucked them into a packet and put them in her bag. Then, after applying a bandage to the needle prick area, she pulled up a chair and sat down next me. "How long has it been since your parents died?"

"A little over two years. Come December, it will have been three years since I moved back to Moonshadow Bay. Why? Do you think this has to do with their deaths?"

Linda shook her head. "Not really. But that was a major

stressor in your life. And a few months later you got into a new relationship. You had just gotten out of a bad relationship that lasted, what, eighteen years? You started a new job that—for the last three years—has not only put you in danger on a physical level, but also psychic and magical levels. Even if you're enjoying your life, January, your stress level has to be off the scale. And just a few days ago, you lost one of your few remaining relatives. I'm thinking that you may be suffering from burnout or overwhelm, or both."

I hadn't thought of it that way, but when she laid it out for me, it did seem like a lot to deal with. "I didn't think it was so intense. I've just been living my life—and I love my life."

"I'm not saying that you don't. What I'm saying is that everything that's happened has had more of an impact on you than you think it has. Sometimes we get so used to running on adrenaline that it seems normal, but that can burn us out. In fact, that can burn out your adrenal glands after a while. And witchblood or not, you have a similar makeup to humans. The fact that you've joined a gym and are working out is good, but even *that* can put more stress on the psyche and body. Especially if you're not used to it."

I stared at my hands. I knew she was right—I had undergone a great deal of stress over the past few years, and it wasn't looking likely to slow down anytime in the future. Especially with the unknown factors of owing the Fae a favor and owing the Crow Man a favor. I hadn't even told the doctor about that part of it.

"There's more," I said, deciding that I'd better tell her everything so we could get an accurate diagnosis. I told her about the trip to search for Bigfoot, and about running into the Crow Man, and running into the Fae and what I had promised both of them.

By the time I finished, Linda was sitting back, her hands on her tablet as she just stared at me.

"*Okay then*, add in two more *major* stressors. And you wonder why you're tired and jumpy, and why you had a migraine? All right, I'm going to go run tests. As I said, no work until next week. And if you're still feeling overwhelmed by then, you need to take more time off. I know Tad well enough to know that he can spare you for a few weeks if need be. And I know him well enough to know that he would. He's one of the best bosses out there."

I couldn't argue with her there. Tad was an excellent supervisor, and he only wanted the best for everybody. "All right. Call me when you get the results."

She stood, motioning for me to stay on the bed. "I'll let myself out. Try not to worry, and try to enjoy yourself. Try to do something that energizes you instead of taking it out of you. I want to see you again on Sunday before I release you for work on Monday." As she hefted her bag over her shoulder and headed for the door, I carefully stood, and made my way for the bathroom after saying good-bye.

I WAS WEARING A COMFORTABLE GAUZE DRESS, LIGHTLY belted, and I was sitting at the table eating the breakfast that Killian had made for me when Ari called. I set down my fork and answered.

"Hey, girl. What's up? This better be good for interrupting waffles and strawberries!"

"I think *you* need to tell *me* what's up. I heard through the grapevine that you ended up fainting at work yesterday?"

The rumor mill worked fast in a town as small as Moonshadow Bay. "Yes, actually, it's true. I was going to call you later and tell you. I've been so busy the past few days that I haven't had time to even think."

"I talked to Tad. I stopped in at your office to see if you

wanted to go to lunch today, and you weren't there. They told me everything. So what the hell happened?"

"It was bad. And we're not sure what brought it on but—" I paused as my call waiting beeped. Teran was on the other line. "Hey, my aunt's on the other line and I should probably talk to her first. Can I call you back in about ten minutes?"

"Of course you can. But you'd better make sure you do or I'm coming over there." As Ari hung up, I answered Teran's call.

"Hey, what's up?" I was hoping that Teran wouldn't have heard already. It was so much easier to break news before somebody else elaborated on it. But I was out of luck there, as well.

"I gather that you had an incident yesterday? Are you all right? I'm coming over there to help take care of you. Are you at Killian's right now?" She spoke so quickly I couldn't get a word in edgewise to answer any of her questions.

"Yes, I had an incident—a sudden, debilitating migraine. Yes, I'm all right. And yes, I'm at Killian's. Are you sure you want to spend your afternoon over here?" I was beginning to realize that I didn't like being fussed over. I made a terrible patient.

"Yes, I'm coming over. I'll be there in half an hour. Is Killian there?"

"Yes, he's right here." I grimaced, wondering if all of my close friends were going to be like this. "It was just a migraine, for fuck's sake. It was nothing."

"Oh, it was *nothing*? You collapsed in front of your coworkers and it was *nothing*?"

I groaned, pinching the bridge of my nose. "I didn't collapse. Not exactly. I'll tell you when you get here. Drive slowly—there's no need to hurry. Killian is right here and he's watching over me. I'm eating breakfast now and would like to finish my waffle before it gets cold."

But before I could even say good-bye, Teran had hung up and I knew she was on the way. I called Ari back, sighing as I eyed my waffle. It was going to get cold. I glanced over at Killian he silently took it from me and popped it in the microwave for a few seconds to heat it up.

"All right, why don't you come over if you've got the time?" I said when Ari answered. "Teran is on the way, and it's easier to tell both of you what happened at the same time, rather than repeat the story endlessly."

"I'll be there. And I'm bringing cheesecake." Ari hung up.

I glanced over at Killian. "Honestly, everyone acts like I had a seizure or split my head on the sidewalk or something like that. I just had a migraine and it knocked me out for a moment."

Killian settled down at the table, a serious look on his face. "I think you should take a leave of absence from work until after our wedding. I know you don't want to hear that, but with everything you've been through in the past few years, and the stress of planning our wedding, I'm worried that it might take its toll on you. And don't talk to me about how strong you are. I know you're a strong-willed woman, and I know you can handle one hell of a lot, but even the strongest person needs help at times, or down time, or both."

I toyed with my waffle and then dug in. I didn't know what to say. I wanted to argue, but Killian was worried about me. And to be honest, if the same thing had happened to him, I'd be just as worried.

He was waiting for an answer, though, so after I finished my waffle, I pushed my plate back and reached across the table to take his hand.

"I know you love me and I know you're worried about me. And I know Ari's worried about me, and Teran is worried about me, and my coworkers are worried about me. But all of this worrying about me is just making me *more* stressed.

Rowan and I are going down to talk to Gretchen. If we can get her to remove the curse then it's all going to be fine."

"And what if Gretchen says no? What if she's not there? What will you do then?" He squeezed my hand hard, not letting go.

I leaned back, trying to keep an even temper. "Then maybe we'll approach the Court Magika like Rowan suggested. Or maybe Hank's friend will come through— apparently he has a very powerful witchblood friend who might be able to remove the curse. I don't know. I can't tell you until we find out what does happen. And I'm going to stress even worse if I speculate."

"I take it you want me to let it go for now?"

I nodded. "I *need* you to let it go for now. It's been an odd week, a stressful week. I feel like I suddenly entered some bizarro world. Not only are two cases hanging at work because of me, but I'm trying to navigate my feelings about my grandmother and this curse. In some ways I wish Esmara had told me about it earlier, although I guess that wouldn't have helped, either."

Killian slowly let out his breath, released my fingers and sat back. "All right, my love. I'll stop nagging at you. But I wish you'd consider what the doctor said and take some leave. You know Tad will hold your job for you."

My stomach knotted at the thought. But I reluctantly nodded. "I can't promise to do that, but I promise I'll think about it. I don't know what I'd do if I stayed home."

"You're always talking about wanting to write some short stories. Or what about a novel? You're a writer at heart. I know you miss the magazine even though you never say so." He pointed toward my plate "Would you like another waffle?"

I was going to say no, but then I shrugged. "What the hell? I might as well. I could eat a dozen of them, but I know that wouldn't be good for me."

As he moved to make more waffles, I looked around the kitchen. This wasn't *my* kitchen, but it felt like home. The floors were gray laminate, but they looked just like wood. The kitchen was painted a pale blue, and had updated appliances. There was a chef's range, two massive wall ovens, a state-of-the-art refrigerator and dishwasher, and beautiful quartz counters. I tried to imagine what it would be like to live here, to make this my home instead of the house I had grown up in. It was hard to envision, and yet—Killian lived here, and because he was here, this had the feel of home to it.

"Do you mind if I look around the house today? I mean really look at it?"

"Of course, go ahead. But why?" He brought over the waffles and set them down next to the bowl of sliced berries and real maple syrup.

"Because if I decide to live here, I have to figure out how to make it my home as well." I glanced at him, waiting.

"So you might decide to move in?" There was hope in his voice, but he kept it low-key.

"Possibly. If I can make some changes to make it feel like my home too." I stabbed another waffle and put it on my plate, drowning it with butter and syrup and strawberries. I added a big dollop of whipped cream on top, deciding that I was already on sugar overload. It couldn't hurt to add more.

"There are only a few things I would object to changing," Killian said. "My office stays my office. But if you wanted to take the den for your office, you could change it however you wanted. I'm not fond of the color pink. I'd prefer that our bedroom not be pink. I can handle purple, I can handle green, blue—that's fine. But not pink. Also, the basement is finished, and it's big enough we could divvy it up. I can have my side to invite the guys over for games. You can have the other side for your ritual room. My side would stay paneled, your side would be yours to decorate as you so choose."

I grinned at that. "Is that all?"

"No. I want the bedroom to feel like our sanctuary. The kitchen's been recently renovated and I'd like to keep it this way. I love the dark cabinets and the white quartz and the gray floors. As far as the living room goes, I'm willing to give up the leather sofas if you want to bring over your microfiber set. That's comfortable and I know you love it. You're welcome to make it more feminine in whatever way you choose. But I'd rather not keep potpourri around because the smell bothers me unless it's more cinnamon oriented and less floral."

Wolf shifters had notoriously strong senses of smell, and they often had adverse reactions to floral perfumes and citrus scents. I had changed my perfume to a spicy musky blend because he liked it better and didn't sneeze when he smelled it.

"As long as we can have fresh flowers in there?"

"I love fresh flowers. And that's a good compromise. So, do you think you want to move in? We can rent your house out and keep it in your name." He paused, then added, "Also, if you want to keep your last name, I'm good with that. I understand the importance of heritage."

I nodded. Even though the Jaxsons were my step-grandparents, they were still a link to my father. And they had been part of my life. And while O'Connell was a fine name, I had always been January Jaxson, and it was hard for me to imagine giving it up.

"I do want to keep my last name." I hesitated, then decided just to go for it. "All right, this house is a lot bigger than mine. We can take down the fence between the two and have a huge lot. I'd love to create a little orchard out back, and a big vegetable garden. As far as renting out my house, what about turning it into a guesthouse? We could scale it down, and then use it when we have company."

Killian laughed. "When are we going to have company that needs a guesthouse? I understand not wanting to rent it out to strangers. But I don't want to tear it down. It means so much to you because it was your childhood home, and it's a link to your parents."

I stabbed another bite of the waffle, then finally sat back and looked at him. "We can figure out what to do with my house later. There's no rush. But I'd like to get started on some renovations here before our wedding. Maybe if I take some time off, I can paint and redecorate some of the rooms."

Killian's eyes began to shine. "Does that mean you're moving in with me when we get married, Ms. Jaxson?"

I laughed, it was good to see him look so happy. "I suppose it does, Mr. O'Connell."

At that moment, the doorbell rang. Killian went to answer as I went back to my waffle, feeling better now that I'd taken one big decision off the table. And truthfully, maybe it was a good idea for me to make some changes. Maybe I was living inside my memories by holding onto the house in which I had grown up. Feeling satisfied, even though my head was still foggy, I went back to my waffle as Killian escorted both Ari and Teran in. They were followed by Rowan, and I realize that we were going to have quite the little tribunal once we finished breakfast.

CHAPTER FIFTEEN

*K*illian kept all three of them from descending on me at once. He held up his hand before they could say anything, and brought his finger to his lips.

"January still has a headache, so fawn over her all you want but keep it down, please."

I whispered *Thank you* to him, and he winked at me.

"Now, I'm going to put on coffee and tea, there are cookies in the cupboard and we still have tasting cake left, which should be eaten up soon. I'll leave you four to talk." As he put on the kettle for tea and then began making a pot of coffee, Teran sat down next to me.

She looked at me, concern written all over her face. "I'm not sure how what we've heard jives with what really happened. So why don't you tell us everything, as best as you can, before we assume the worst."

I filled them in on everything that had happened the past couple days. I left nothing out: the argenium worms, the Shoners' house, the graveyard garden and the body in the hole. Which reminded me, I wanted to talk to Millie about what was going on. I had promised not to do any work, but that didn't mean I couldn't ask questions. I also told them what Esmara had said about the strange energy in my aura and the curse, and what Dr. Fairsight had confirmed.

Teran let out a long sigh. "I should have told you about that sooner. I knew it was in your aura. It was there when you were young, and it's still there now. I just hoped that maybe we'd find a way out of this before I'd have to say anything."

"I just want it over with," I said. "I actually asked Esmara why nobody in the family did anything about this before. She had some good answers, but I think if I thought my daughter was going to be affected by a curse, I'd search high and low for the person who cast it. I can't say I'm feeling very friendly toward our ancestors right now."

Ari worried her lip. "I just can't believe that someone could cast a curse that would last this long. I'll go with you if you want to hunt her down. You know I've got your back."

"Rowan and I are going down to Seattle tomorrow. We found out where she lives, and we're going to confront her."

"I'll come with if you want me to. I can actually cast a pretty hefty punch when I want to." Ari reached out and took my hand, squeezing tightly. "Nobody messes with my bestie and gets away with it."

"I'd love to have you come with us. That's okay, isn't it?" I turned to Rowan.

"In this case, backup would be welcome. But I beg of you—don't go off the rails, either one of you. We want to gain her cooperation, not drive a wedge in the situation. By now she may have gotten all she needs out of the curse. If not, she may ask for something in return that we aren't prepared to give."

Rowan shooed Killian away from the counter and took over making the tea. Teran got out mugs, as well as the tasting cakes. Rowan poured the water over the tea bags in the flowered teapot, then brought both it and the coffee pot to the table. She poured coffee for me, tea for herself and Ari, and Teran foraged in the refrigerator for a soda. I decided I wanted some of the lemon blueberry cake, and sliced the tasting cakes in half, divvying them up.

"I admit, the migraine scared the hell out of me. I've never had a headache quite that bad, and it's lingering today. I don't know whether this is because of the curse, because of stress, or maybe I'm sick, or maybe it's something else. The doctor took some blood today and she's going to run some tests. I don't know if this is a one-off, but it scared the hell out of me." I paused, shaking my head, but quickly stopped because even that hurt.

"Well, I can tell you that migraines don't run in our family," Teran said. "Headaches, occasionally, but everyone gets a headache now and then. I hope they don't find anything too out of place." She paused, then said, "I feel like I should go with you tomorrow as well. The curse affects me just as much as it affects you, and I feel like a coward doing nothing about it. I just never knew much about what went on. You'd think my mother would have told me more than she did." Teran sounded hurt. In fact, the look in her eyes told me that something about this had stabbed her deeply.

"Tell me, if you feel up to it, what went on between you and your mother? Esmara has hinted that things weren't right between you." I wasn't sure if I should ask, but matters being what they were, I felt like we needed to be as clear as we could with each other.

Teran finished off her cake and then took a long sip of her tea. She glanced at Ari, then at Rowan. "I suppose I might as well tell all of you. My mother's dead now, so it's not going to make any difference. Even when she finally *is* able to contact me, all she can do is yell from the other side."

"Does it have something to do with what I did with your fiancé?" Rowan asked, surprisingly quietly.

Teran shook her head. "No, and please know that was long ago, and I'm actually grateful to you for exposing to me what he really was. I don't hold any form of a grudge about it. And my mother didn't either. She didn't like you because she knew that you and her mother were...*close*... And that wasn't considered proper back then."

I glanced at Rowan. "Let's have it out on the table. You had a thing for my great-grandmother, right?" I also knew that she had helped my great-grandmother kill a serial killer and hide him in the woods, but I decided to keep that quiet for now. I wasn't sure whether Teran actually knew about it, and it wasn't my place to bring that knowledge out into the open.

Rowan closed her eyes for a moment, and a look of sadness passed over her face. "Colleen and I grew very close. At first she thought I was after Brian, but that wasn't the truth at all. I actually found him annoying and he did his best to keep her from her true potential. He was always envious of her, because she had a greater power than he did. He treated her well, overall, but he just sort of...*muffled* her."

"I always wondered about that," Teran said. "My mother used to talk about my grandfather as being stern and overly patriarchal for being witchblood."

"He was. It was more out of insecurity than anything else. Anyway, after Colleen and I got to know one another, we bonded over some fairly intense happenings. One included your aunt Lara—the sister who died young. But let's leave that alone for now. I would drop by to chat with Colleen every now and then because she was lonely. Bluntly put, she was stuck with a passel of kids, and although she was revered as the mother of Moonshadow Bay, she didn't have many friends. The women in town either envied her for her place or they were intimidated by her power. Colleen was exceptionally strong in her magic and I seemed to be the only one who recognized it. I encouraged her to use her powers, and Brian grew suspicious. He didn't seem to even consider that we would find each other romantically attractive, but he was concerned that I'd encourage her to expand her powers. That would have made him even more insecure."

"Was my grandmother happy?" Teran asked.

"She was happy when we talked. I treated her with the respect that she never received from her husband, and unlike the women of town, I wanted to be her friend. We would go out walking for hours at a time. Sometimes we'd take the kids and let them run and play, other times they would stay home and Trixie, who was the oldest, would watch after the others." Rowan paused again, and her eyes glistened.

"Was she in love with you?" I asked.

"*We* were in love. I'll be honest, we did have an affair. It lasted for about two years until Brian walked in on us one day. He never said anything, as far as I know, but after that day it was over. Colleen and I remained friendly but I never again came over when she was alone. I didn't want Brian to take it out on her, and back then—even amid the Otherkin—same-sex relationships weren't exactly approved. At least, not here in America. There were parts in Europe where we would've been just fine, but it just wasn't something we could continue."

I glanced at Teran. She didn't look angry, or even appalled. In fact, I thought she looked relieved.

"Thank you for trying to make my grandmother's life a little better." Teran reached for another piece of cake. "And thank you for helping my niece."

"Don't forget, January's also my granddaughter. What an interesting little web we have woven here amongst us." Rowan leaned back, crossed one leg over the other. "I never met another woman I thought I could love. And then of course, I fell for Farlow Bell, who was also married. And of course that didn't work out, but I'd never take it back, because it eventually resulted in January entering my life. I wish I could have brought up my son, but things happen for a reason."

"And now you're getting it on with a Funtime demon," I said, trying to lighten the mood. The energy had grown incredibly thick as she talked, and I wondered if Esmara was hanging around listening.

"How is that going, by the way?" Ari asked. "Any wedding bells in the future?"

Rowan laughed, breaking the tension. "I don't think so. I'm fond of Tarvish and he's fond of me, and he's an extremely good lover. Go figure. But I don't see us walking down the aisle. No, I don't think I am fated to marry, and that's fine with me."

Teran held up her teacup. "Here, here! I totally agree with you. And now, since Rowan shared her secrets, I'll tell you what was wrong between me and my mother. I never want you to think badly of her, January. My mother was a good woman, for the most part. But she never forgave me for not giving her a grandchild. She called me selfish, and I think you'll be surprised when they probate her will."

"Why?" I asked.

"I know for a fact that, while she's left me certain mementos, she's willed everything else to you. She told me years ago that if I couldn't—no, if I *wouldn't*—give her a grandchild, then I wasn't inheriting anything from her. My mother really believed that I owed her an heir. She always compared me to Althea, in terms of getting married and having children. And when I complained about how Althea never taught you about your heritage, while she agreed with me that it was wrong, she used that to hammer me even more. She wanted an heir who could fully use her powers."

"Naomi was *really* that old-fashioned?" Rowan asked. "I'll

bet you that she blamed me for the fact that you broke your engagement to that cad. What was his name?"

"Caine Rogers. And while she didn't blame you, she did blame *me* for not overlooking what he did. She said that it was a woman's duty to provide heirs for the family, and I had decided to be selfish in my choice not to marry and have children. When I pointed out that she already had a grandchild, her response was 'You never know when someone's going to die, so there needs to be more than one to carry on the legacy.' "

"You mean she wrote you out of her will simply because you chose to stay unattached?" In some ways it didn't surprise me, but on the other hand it seemed incredibly shortsighted for a woman as strong as Naomi had been. "She probably would have tried to encourage me to have children."

"Oh, trust me, she was planning to hound you. She told me that, if she couldn't change my mind, maybe she could change yours. No, I doubt there's going to be any change when the lawyers contact us." She shrugged. "I accepted it when she told me. I'm not going to put up any fuss, so don't worry about that."

I stared at her, stunned. How could my grandmother be so incredibly shortsighted and cruel? There was no way on earth that I'd accept the inheritance and leave Teran out in the cold. Right then, I knew that I was going to turn every penny over to her, because she needed it, and it was rightfully hers. She must have read the look on my face because she teared up.

"Now do you understand why I am so conflicted in terms of my mother's death? I loved her but I always knew that she didn't approve of me. She didn't approve of my lifestyle, of my choices, and she always favored your mother over me. I didn't blame Althea for it, though. It wasn't her fault that our mother played favorites."

I glanced over at Ari. She looked slightly uncomfortable, and I realized that she felt like she might be intruding on family matters. Even though she was my bestie and I would have told her everything anyway. I decided to change the subject.

"So tomorrow, the four of us are going down to see Gretchen. What's our plan of attack? I mean, do we just go up and knock on her door and say excuse me, you set a curse on our family that's been killing our women for hundreds of years and would you please take it off before the two of us die too soon?" I grimaced. I could just imagine how well that would go over.

"Do you even know if the woman is still sane? I mean, really, when you're that vindictive and you pass out curses for money, I think it tends to wear on you a little bit," Ari said.

"Unfortunately, I don't think we're going to know what we're up against until we get there," Rowan said. "I tried to do some research over the past couple weeks, and frankly, there isn't much about her out there on the internet. She doesn't seem to be aligned with any organization that I can tell, and if she's still doing what she used to, there's no sign of that, either. I'm not sure what to think."

"I think we just have to go knock on her door and play it by ear," Teran said. "It's been a long time. I wonder if she even remembers who Ellen was. If Gretchen was used to casting curses for a living, wouldn't it be kind of like trying to remember one tarot client from a hundred years ago or more? Not everybody stands out."

"You know, I have to agree with Teran," Rowan said. "We'll just play it by ear. And hopefully she'll be either intimidated enough by us or she just won't care anymore. Val Slater has given me a notarized document indicating that he wants to call off the vendetta. His grandfather's no longer alive so Val can speak for his family. If nothing else, that should help.

Plus, I'm ready to offer her a hefty price to break the spell if she won't do it any other way. She took money to cast it, she might take money to break it."

And on that note, my head began to hurt again. "Let's put this conversation to rest for now. I just want to relax, and I'd love to have company, if you don't mind just sitting in the living room, watching a movie or something gentle."

Rowan had to get back to her house, and Teran was teaching an adult education class on gardening so she had to go. But Ari said she'd stay with me. She saw the others out, then helped me into the living room where I stretched out in the recliner. I grabbed her hand.

"Thank you for being here today. It's been a rough past week. And finding out how Nonny felt about Teran makes it even more difficult. I feel so conflicted."

Ari wandered into the kitchen and brought back a bottle of water for me, along with some more of the tasting cakes. One was blackberry white chocolate, and the other was orange and vanilla. She handed me a plate with a portion of each on it and took a plate for herself over to the sofa where she curled up.

"I understand. My sister and I are still dealing with our feelings about our half-brother. We haven't met yet, but we're planning on driving up in December to say hello. Actually, we're meeting him in Seattle, sort of halfway between Terameth Lake and Moonshadow Bay. Why is family so damned complicated?"

I shrugged, diving into the cake. The sugar probably wasn't good for me, but right now I didn't care. "I have no clue. Oh, in other news—because other news sounds really good compared to what we've been talking about—I've decided to move in with Killian. I'm going to redecorate some of the rooms in my style."

"Really? You're leaving your parents' house? I thought you loved that house."

"I do, but last night I realized it's not practical. We need more room, I know that. And there was no way I could make it up to my bedroom in the shape I was in. It helps to have a bedroom on the ground floor in case something like this happens again. We can rent out my house, or turn it into a vacation rental or something like that. I don't know, but I do know that this seems like the right move. It just feels right in my heart. I'm kind of excited about it. And Killian's over the moon."

"If you're happy about it, and he's happy about it, then that's all that matters. Listen, I have a thought. I am actually thinking of moving my salon out of the house. Once we have a child, we don't want strangers in the house with our children. So maybe it's time I find a place that I can turn into a salon. Would you object to me renovating your house into a full-scale salon?"

I stared at her. "Are you serious?"

"I think I am. I can rent someplace if you're not interested, but it would be fun to work next door to you. I'm pretty sure I could get the zoning requirements approved. I make a good income now and I've been thinking about expanding the business. You know, hiring on some new hairstylists, maybe a skin care consultant and a makeup artist? I could open a complete beauty salon if I had a full house to work with."

My heart leaped. If Ari took over my parents' house and turned it into a place where women could go to feel beautiful and relaxed, that would be wonderful.

"I'd like to hire a nail tech, and as I said, I have a friend who runs yoga classes out of her house and I'm sure she would love to have a space to offer them. I've actually been thinking about this for a while, but I haven't even told Meagan."

"You think she'd try to talk you out of it?"

"No, on the contrary," Ari said. "She would encourage me to do it, and I don't have anything concrete to show yet. Just a few ideas." Her eyes were bright, and I could tell that she was excited.

"Do you want to *buy* the house? If you did, I'd be willing to sell but I want to keep most of the backyard. Killian and I want to plant an orchard out there and gardens." This could be the perfect solution. And Ari would be right next door so we'd see each other more often.

"I don't need much more than a strip for parking. Let me see what City Hall has to say about zoning regulations. I can ask. It doesn't mean we have to go through with it if you change your mind."

Feeling cheerful for the first time in days, I took another bite of cake and rubbed my forehead. "Go ahead. Check it out and get back to me. I'd love to have you next door, even if it's for your job." In a way, it would kind of be like when we were kids and she lived right up the block. Oh sure, it would be different, but even if I saw her every day to say hello, it would make the world a brighter place. "I sure love you, I hope you know that."

"And I love you too. You're my bestie. We've been best friends since childhood, and I see us being best friends until the end of our days. Okay, what do you want to watch?" She picked up the remote.

We settled on watching something calming and easy on my eyes, a show about Cornwall, England. As we settled back, cake and water in hand, it occurred to me that—despite the ghosts and headaches and family issues—I was one of the luckiest women in the world. And I never wanted to forget that.

CHAPTER SIXTEEN

That evening, Killian ordered takeout and we ate in bed. "Are you ready for tomorrow?" Killian asked.

I shrugged. "As ready as I'll ever be. I wish we had done this years ago, but I didn't know about it then."

"How are you feeling?" He handed me the container of potstickers. We had curled up in the guestroom bed with the cats, and we were watching *Terminator 2*, still one of the best action movies ever made.

"Scared. Worried. I'm not sure what the doctor is going to find out. And then...what if Gretchen refuses to help and we can't convince her? What if she isn't there anymore and we've blown our chance? I don't even want to think about that because there are so many possible outcomes, and a lot of them are bad. Can we just watch the movie?" I didn't want to talk about it. I didn't want to talk about anything that had happened because it was so problematic.

Killian wrapped his arm around my shoulders and we went back to eating dinner and watching Arnold right the wrongs of the world.

THE NEXT MORNING I DRESSED IN A COBALT BLUE LINEN skirt and lavender V-neck sweater. As I buckled my silver belt around my waist and zipped up my knee-high boots, I was trying my best to keep out of the panic spiral. My head felt better, but my anxiety was sky high. I told Killian to go to work.

"It's going to take us a couple hours' drive down there anyway, and then who knows what's going to happen. Go take care of kitties and doggies and make them happy and healthy. I'll text you when we get there." I bit into the sausage muffin sandwich he had made me for breakfast, and hurried out to wait on the front porch. We'd grab coffee on the way. A few minutes after nine, Rowan pulled up, driving her new SUV. Ari and Teran were in the back, and I dashed down the stairs and slid into the front passenger seat.

I glanced over at Rowan and let out a long sigh. "Let's get this over with."

"Coffee first?" Rowan asked.

"Always." As I turned around to greet Teran and Ari, I tried to ignore the rumble of thunder overhead. The roads would be slick today, rife with rain puddles, and I whispered a quick prayer to Druantia for safety in our journey. Rowan eased away from the curb, and we stopped at the local espresso stand before we hit the freeway.

ON A DAY WITH MODERATE TRAFFIC, THE TRIP TO SEATTLE from Moonshadow Bay took around two hours. At least at a moderate speed, it did. If the traffic was heavy it could take up to three or four hours, and with the best conditions, a little over ninety minutes.

Bellingham was close to the northern border of Washington state, and Seattle was farther south, along Puget Sound. We had missed the worst of rush-hour traffic, but we still hit the last of the trickle. Near Everett we slowed, thanks to a military convoy heading into the naval shipyard, but once we passed the area, we sped up again.

The roads north of Seattle seemed wide open and spacious, with Puget Sound on one side and farmland on the other. But as we neared Seattle, everything started getting congested again. I glanced at the clock. We had been on the road for not quite two hours, so we'd actually made fairly good time.

The entire time on the road, we had been quiet—all of us. A little small talk here and there, but nothing of any substance. Teran and I had the most to lose from this trip, but I knew that both Ari and Rowan were worried as well. Not to mention the fact that they were headed into a meeting with a very powerful witch and if she decided they were troublemakers, she could cause a lot of trouble for *them*, as well.

As the skyscrapers began to appear on both sides of the freeway, I glanced at Rowan. "Where does she live?"

"In North Seattle. She actually lives in Shoreline, so we need to take exit 176." Rowan's voice sounded as tense as I felt. She flipped on her right-turn signal and we shifted into the exit lane, following the ramp to where it intersected North 175th Street.

Once there, Rowan merged into the right-hand lane. We continued on for two blocks until we came to the junction where the road intersected with Meridian Avenue North. We waited in the right-hand turn lane for the lights to change, and then—turning right again—we traveled half a block until we came to N. 176th Street.

Once again we turned right, and then, after two houses, left onto Bagley Place.

Bagley Place was a cul-de-sac, and Rowan slowed as we came to a green house with a blue metal roof. It looked odd amid the other houses, all of which had beige siding and light brown roofs. All of the houses looked to have been built at the same time, common among the developments in Seattle.

Rowan pulled into the driveway of house number 17610, parking behind an old green pickup truck. The neighborhood didn't look pricey, but neither did it look rundown. It looked like the kind of neighborhood where you'd find kids running up and down the road, riding their skateboards around, and where a new car for a neighbor would be cause for a party.

"Is this it?" I asked. I don't know what I'd been expecting, but it hadn't been a suburban split-level house. Maybe I'd expected something more like Rowan's cottage, with the yard filled full of witchy plants. Or maybe I'd expected an old brownstone, four stories up in a fading apartment building.

"Yeah, this is it. This neighborhood tends to be shifter oriented, so it's odd that she would pick here to live. But here we are." She turned off the car and sat back, staring at the house. "Before we converge on her doorstep, let's discuss how we introduce ourselves."

"I guess… Introduce ourselves as Ellen ó Broin's descendants? At least Teran and me? We can see if that jogs her memory?" Now that we were here, my nerves had settled. There was nothing left to do except go in and see what happened. "I thought I'd be more nervous than I am. I was a bundle of anxiety this morning. But here I am, calm as a cucumber." I held up my hand. I wasn't shaking at all.

"Sometimes, facing the dragon is easier than thinking about the confrontation. All right, let's get the show on the road. If she gets nasty, leave it to me." Rowan opened her door and, shouldering her purse, stepped out on the pavement. The rest of us followed. She and I led the way up to the door, where—after hesitating for just a second—I rang the bell.

There was no answer at first, so I rang it again.

"All right, all right, I'm coming. Hold your horses," came a crotchety voice from inside.

I caught my breath, my nerves flooding back. Ari reached around and held my hand, which helped. Teran put her hand on my shoulder.

The door creaked open, and a woman peeked out. To my surprise, she looked no older than Rowan herself, even though she had to be at least a hundred years older. She stared at us for a moment, looking suspicious, then opened the door a little wider.

"What do you want?" The voice was a lot older than the vision in front of us.

I glanced at Rowan, who nodded for me to go ahead. "Are you Gretchen Wyer?"

"That's my name, don't wear it out. Who are you? And why do you want to know?"

"My name is January Jaxson. My great-great-grandmother was Ellen ó Broin. You put a hex on her along with all the women in my family. Do you remember?"

For a moment, the vision in front of us wavered and I thought I could see an old, gnarled woman standing there. Then what was obviously an illusion stabilized again. Gretchen stood there, just staring at us, not moving to close the door or open it either.

"It would be helpful if you let us in," I said. "We need to talk."

"You're not going to let this go, are you?" Gretchen asked.

At that, I wanted to roll my eyes. But I refrained. "No, we're not letting this go. This is my aunt Teran behind me, my paternal grandmother, Rowan Firesong, and my friend Ari. Please let us in."

Another moment passed before Gretchen finally opened the door and stood back. As we entered the house, I was surprised by how clean and tidy it was. Again, I had expected cobwebs and dried herbs everywhere, everything you would think of in a typical *old witch of the woods* lair. But the house looked almost minimalistic.

Gretchen led us into the living room and motioned for us to sit down. Another moment, and the illusion dissolved. We found ourselves facing a hunched-over old gnome of a woman with a knot on her back. She barely reached five feet. She didn't have the stereotypical warts, but her hair was in a messy bun on top of her head, and her face looked like it had more ridges on it than a topographical map of a mountain range.

Teran and I sat on the sofa, while Ari sat in a wing chair, and Rowan sat on a large ottoman. Gretchen took her place in her rocking chair. It had a throw over the back and on the table beside it was a plate of milk and cookies. I had a flashback to the story of Little Red Riding Hood, wondering if she was a wolf in sheep's clothing. I'd been prepared for a tall nightmare of a woman with lightning bolts surging around her. I certainly hadn't expected someone who looked like somebody's nana.

"I wondered if I would ever hear from any of Ellen's descendants," Gretchen said. "I've waited for this day for a long time."

I glanced at Rowan, worried. Was she about to unleash hell on our heads? Was she going to start shooting fireballs our way? Or was she going to offer us a plate of poisoned cookies or apples?

"A lot of women in my family have died far too early because of you." I held Gretchen's gaze, or tried to. Her eyes swirled with energy, and I realized that, little old lady or not, Gretchen was still one of the most powerful witches around.

"I know," she said. "I'm not even going to bother to apologize. I did what I did because that's who I was back then. Trust me, far more families than yours have come to a bad end because of me."

She was so unemotional in her speech that she was unreadable. Was she proud? Did she regret it? Did it even matter to her anymore?

"We need you to remove the curse," Rowan said, stepping in. "It's time to lay it to rest."

"Well, at least you came in time. Another few months and you'd be too late." Gretchen leaned back in her rocking chair, picking up one of the cookies off the table. She bit into it, then let out a sigh. "There's a season for everything, and the Wheel never stops turning."

Teran cleared her throat and leaned forward. "You're dying?"

"We're *all* dying," Gretchen said. "Some die young, some die late. But all of us die. Except the Fae—they only die when they're killed. And the gods. And some of the nature spirits. So I suppose not everything dies, but those of us who are of mortal blood do. There are so many curses I've placed around the world in my time. I don't remember many of them. I do remember Ellen's, though. That was one of the few curses I've ever regretted. I needed the money so I carried through, but I never forgot it because Ellen was a remarkable woman, and she would have been more powerful than I was, had I not placed the hex on her line."

"I'm curious. Did you believe that she hexed Slater's cattle or crops, or whatever it was he accused her of?" Teran asked.

Gretchen laughed. "Oh, no. It wasn't *she* who cursed his crops. I had to drum up business, you see. And I made it *my* business to know who didn't like whom. Once I found conflict, it was easy enough to create the illusion that neighbor X screwed over neighbor Y. *Especially* back then. And especially when old man Slater had a thing for Ellen and she didn't return it."

"Slater wanted her?" I asked, cringing. Val hadn't mentioned that.

"Oh, he slobbered over her. He was a pudgy puffy old man and he saw her beauty, and all he could think about was getting his hands on her. But Ellen's father refused his offers to marry the girl, regardless of how much clout it would have brought the family. Slater liked his spirits. He liked his food too much, too. So it was easy enough for me to plant the idea in his head that Ellen was the one who had cursed his crops."

I stared at her, amazed that she could be so ruthless. "You actually double-crossed my great-great-grandmother for *money*? And not only her, but every woman who bears her blood?"

"As I told you, I was younger then. It was hard to make a living, especially in a world that really didn't appreciate women, especially women like *us*. At times it was kill or be killed. Only I chose to do my killing in a way that profited me without laying the blame at my feet."

I hated to admit it, but she had a good point.

"I dropped a hint in Slater's ear that Ellen was out to make a fool of him, and to impoverish him. He asked me to make her regret it. I convinced him that a curse of that proportion would be the worst thing that could happen to her. And then I charged him a small fortune. But because I could ensure that her descendants would never be happy, he agreed to my price. He was a petty, greedy man."

Gretchen's delivery confused me. On one hand, I had the feeling she regretted casting the hex. On the other, she seemed so matter-of-fact about it.

"Would you be willing to remove the curse?" Teran asked.

Gretchen looked her straight in the eyes. "I have perhaps a month left on this earth. I've seldom done anything for anyone's benefit, except my own. But now? Here at the end? I don't care. Remove it, leave it, it matters not. I will meet my gods and own everything I've done. So, yes. I'll break the curse. If you hadn't arrived, I wouldn't have thought twice about it. But since you're here, I will break the hex."

"What do you need? Better to do it now than wait until you're dead not be able to break it," Rowan said.

I did a double take, surprised she'd be that blunt. But then again, considering who we were dealing with and what she was like, it didn't surprise me after all.

"Come with me." Gretchen stood and shuffled down the hallway. We followed her into what looked like had been a large family room at one point. One wall was covered with an apothecary cabinet, tiny drawers from floor to ceiling. Gretchen worried her lip as she stared up at the wall. "Fourth drawer from the top, third row from the left. If one of you will climb up there and retrieve the scroll that's within that drawer, we can proceed."

Ari pulled a stepstool over and quickly climbed up, barely able to reach the drawer in question. She opened it and retrieved a roll of parchment paper, tied with a string. As she jumped down back to the floor, I gasped. A bolt of energy shot through me the moment I saw the parchment. Teran gasped as well.

"By your reactions, it's apparent this is the right scroll," Gretchen said. "Every drawer in this cabinet contains a scroll of a hex or a spell that I've cast—positive and negative alike. By burning the scrolls, the spells will be broken. As you can see, I've kept my records well." She turned to Rowan and handed her the scroll. "All you have to do is toss it in the fire and it will break the hex. The curse will be lifted."

"All these years—practically a couple centuries—and that's

all it would have taken to keep my great-grandmother and all my great-aunts from dying too young? And my mother?" A sudden wave of anger swept over me. "How could you just keep all these hexes alive? What about all the people who have been impacted over the years? Haven't you ever thought about their lives and what you did to them?"

Rowan placed a hand on my shoulder. "Stop. Just stop."

Gretchen leaned toward me, her gaze holding my own prisoner. Her eyes blazed, even within the gnarled body she now inhabited.

"Girl, you know so little of the world. You have no idea of everything that I've been through in my life, or what I've had to do to stay alive. Every action that we make affects something else. You step on an ant, you destroy that life. You eat a hamburger, and you're eating what was once a living being. Do you wear leather? If you eat vegetables harvested from the fields, mice and other creatures die thanks to the harvesting machines. Have you ever done anything that hurt anybody else?"

"Yes," I said, trying to catch my breath. She was practically vibrating with power. I prayed she wouldn't change her mind.

"What if someone kidnapped your aunt over there, and told you that unless you destroyed a neighbor's life, they'd torture her and killed her slowly? What would you do? Would you let your aunt die a long painful death? Would you destroy your neighbor? What if you could save a dozen lives by giving up your own? Would you make that sacrifice?"

I caught my breath and stepped back, unable to answer. The questions seemed so far off-base compared to what she had done, and yet how did I know that she hadn't faced something like the question about Teran? She had already indicated that some of her spells have been cast for her survival, and I really *didn't* know what she had been through.

"I thought so," she said. "And just so you know, I expected you to show up here today. I got a call from Slater's grandson the other evening."

"Val Slater? What did he want?" I said.

"He threatened to turn me into a vampire if I didn't break the spell for you when you showed up. And if there's one thing I do *not* want, it is to spend immortality in my body now. Every step I take is painful. Every breath, I struggle with. Age isn't the only thing that's caught up with me. The weight of my life is crushing me—the weight of my decisions grinds me down a little bit every day."

"How will we know if it worked?" Ari asked.

"You know about the energy in your aura?"

I nodded. "Yes, I do."

"It will vanish. I guarantee it. And Val asked me to tell you to call him and let him know that the hex is broken. Please do that for me. I truly do not want to be stuck as a vampire. Perhaps if I were still young and beautiful, I might consider it. But not now. I'm ready to jump on the Wheel and go around again."

"Not to mince words, but can we burn this while we're here?" Rowan asked, holding up the scroll. "Just call it a bit of insurance, and then you can watch while January phones Val Slater's assistant and leaves a message about the spell."

"We can do that," Gretchen said. She let us over to a fireplace on the other side of the room and set a candle inside the grate. As she lit the candle, Rowan cast the circle. Gretchen eyed her suspiciously, then shook her head. "I certainly wouldn't want to take you on in a battle of magic. I assume your granddaughter here has inherited your abilities?"

"She has, though they're not developed yet. And if we don't break this fucking spell, they won't ever be."

Once the candle was burning, Gretchen motioned for me to carry the scroll over.

"Should I unroll it?" I asked.

"No, leave it tied. If you unroll it, it will just exacerbate the energy." From her tone, I could tell that Gretchen was telling me the truth. She seemed tired and like she just wanted us to go away.

I leaned forward, holding the scroll over the candle until the ancient parchment caught the flame. It burned brightly, and I held it as long as I could, then dropped it into the ashes on the bottom of the fireplace. As the very last of it began to burn, the flames turned brilliant purple, blazing far higher than they would have if it were just plain paper. I gasped, feeling something racing through my body, and when I turned I saw Teran was down on her knees, looking startled.

My breath felt swept out of my body, sucked out by some astral vacuum. A sharp pain ran through my stomach and I doubled over, falling on my knees beside Teran. For a moment I thought I was dying, that Gretchen had played some horrible joke on us, but then, there was an odd crackle surrounding my aura. I could hear it, and I could see it around Teran as well. The next moment, a sea-green energy, looking like lightning, flowed out of our auras and over to the burning paper. There was a small explosion, enough to knock the candle over, and then the lightning flew up the chimney and vanished.

I rolled over, trying to catch my breath. Ari was down on her knees beside Teran as Rowan knelt beside me and helped me sit up. Both she and Ari were watching us carefully, and at first I wasn't sure why, but then Rowan smiled and nodded.

"It's gone. The energy of the curse is gone from your aura. There's no sign of it."

"Teran, too." Ari glanced over at Rowan. "It's vanished."

As I sat there, I wasn't sure what to think. I felt different, like something that had been with me all my life had vanished. It wasn't good or bad, but just...different.

Taking a deep breath, I looked over at Gretchen. Part of me didn't want to thank her, because she shouldn't have cast the spell in the first place. But finally, I decided that I needed to say it for me—not for her. "Thank you for breaking the hex. Thank you for giving us back our lives the way they should be."

Gretchen sat down in her chair again. "That's the only spell I've ever undone," she said. "And I'm not quite sure what I think about it. But it's done and over with." She looked at us. "All right, I've done what you wanted. Now, call Slater and get him off my back."

I put in a call to Val Slater's assistant and put him on speaker. After Gretchen was satisfied that Val would, indeed, get the message, I asked him to have Val back off—that Gretchen had fulfilled her promise to him.

As soon as I hung up, Gretchen unceremoniously kicked us out of her house. I stood under the late-morning drizzle, feeling that a weight had lifted off my shoulders that I had never known was there.

CHAPTER SEVENTEEN

We sat in the car outside of a Wendy's as one of the cashiers brought out two bags of food. She handed them to us, and left with a sprightly smile. We were all dazed, unsure of what to think about what had just gone down.

"I don't know what I expected, but that wasn't it," Rowan said.

"Me either," I said. "I guess I expected we were going to have a showdown with her. Like some magical battle out of a Dungeons & Dragons movie. On the other hand, she left me breathless. She was just so…nonchalant about that wall of hexes and spells she cast. How many other people have had their lives ruined by her? How many need a hex-breaking spell as much as we did? And if all it takes is to burn the scrolls, why doesn't she go through and just do it before she dies? It may not repair the damage, but it would put an end to it."

"Amen to that," Teran said. "I hate to think of how many families have been impacted by her. Though she said she's cast some helpful spells too. But really... Does that make up for all the damage she's done?"

"One reason I stopped you from confronting her was the fact that she still has a month or so to live, at least according to her, and the last thing you want is for her to repeat that spell and then die off." Rowan opened one of the bags and peeked in, pulling out a burger and fries and handing them back to Ari. She handed Teran a fish sandwich, and then a large chicken nuggets to me. Finally, she pulled out a garden salad for herself. The other bag contained four milkshakes.

"Good thinking. That didn't even occur to me while I was in there. Do you think she'll have second thoughts?" Now that Rowan had mentioned the possibility, I was nervous that maybe Gretchen would decide to reactivate the spell.

"I doubt it. But I'm sure a well-placed word from Val Slater will keep her on the straight and narrow. She really does fear facing immortality stuck in that body, and I don't blame her. She's aged poorly, and it's probably due to all the negative magic she's cast. It has a way of eating away at you, and leaving your body as twisted as your psyche is." Rowan handed around the milkshakes and straws, then let out a sigh as she looked out the window.

"The energy is really gone, isn't it? I can feel that my aura feels different. I still have a headache, though it's not as bad as last night. But it's still there. So I don't think it was the curse causing it." I looked out the window. "I wish that we could have done this before Nonny died. Before my mother died."

"Regrets will get us nowhere. Let's just be grateful that you and Teran and all of your female cousins that you haven't met will live to, hopefully, long and healthy lives." Rowan sounded far away, as though her thoughts were long distant.

"What are you thinking?" I asked.

She closed up her window till it was just cracked open as the rain began to sheet down. "I'm wondering how many Gretchens there are in the world, how many walls are covered with the residue of greed like hers. When she dies, what's going to happen to all the spells in there? I think I should contact the Court Magika about it. Maybe they can intervene and destroy the hexes that are still in effect. Then again, some hexes are necessary. I don't want to be the one in charge of that."

"I don't know if I've ever lived a day in my life without wondering about the curse," Teran said. "And January, for what it's worth, if Nonny hadn't told you, I was going to. You can never know that for sure, but you know I've never lied to you."

"I know. I trust you. I guess today's a success. I don't know why I feel like it isn't, or like it's just another odd day, but maybe it's because of the migraine I had last night. At least with the curse gone, I have that much less stress off my shoulders. I still feel like I should go to work today, or maybe tomorrow. But the doctor said I had to stay home." I popped another nugget into my mouth. After chewing and swallowing, I said, "She said I could come down here today, but she was just...really pushy about me not working this week."

"I like Dr. Fairsight," Teran said. "She knows her stuff. I suppose we should start for home," she added.

As we headed home, we took a detour and drove past the area that had been home to my magazine when I had been married to Ellison. The burned-out shell of the building had been cleaned up, but not rebuilt yet. I stared at the remaining rubble in the lot, thinking that I had spent eighteen years building a successful business that had first been stolen from me, then that went up in flames. Part of the fire was my fault, I had to admit. Maybe it was just as well. Killian had suggested I go back to my writing, not full time but just start playing with it again. And maybe he was right. I needed a creative outlet, and by moving into his house I'd have a complete office to myself. Things were changing, and I was finally realizing the value of change.

As we headed north, the rain poured down around us. But Rowan was a good driver, and during the trip home, the mood was a lot more jovial than it had been headed south.

I realized that my home was no longer in Seattle. I'd left very few ties there except for a few friends that I contacted now and then. No, home was in Moonshadow Bay, in a comfortable house with a man whom I had come to love more than I had ever loved anyone else. And now I was free to plan my future, because regardless of what might come, at least I had the chance for a future.

THAT NIGHT, KILLIAN AND I INVITED ROWAN AND Tarvish, Ari and Meagan, Aunt Teran and her beau Andrew Stark, a professor at Western Washington University who taught quantum physics and who was also witchblood, over for dinner. We made it easy on ourselves and ordered pizzas and tacos, Chinese food and burgers, and set everything on the table to create a buffet.

Xi and Klaus were bounding around the house and I cornered them in the downstairs bedroom, shutting the door so they couldn't run off.

"Listen, Xi. How would you like to live here?" I asked. "Permanently?"

As Xi looked up at me with those wide eyes. *This would be our home? We wouldn't live with you, but with Killian?* She sounded a little frantic.

"No, not at all. I'll be living here, too. When Killian and I get married, I think I'll move here. Would you mind living in this house instead of the one we live in now?"

Xi licked her paw and rubbed her face. *Oh, that's what you mean. As long as we're with you, it doesn't matter where we live. This is a bigger house with more places to play. I don't think Klaus will mind either. Can you shut the door? It's loud out there and though we like everybody, there's too much going on.*

I laughed and reached down to kiss her forehead. "Of course. I'll bring in your dinner soon."

As I stood up, she reached out with one paw and snagged my leg. *Be careful. You're still weak—and vulnerable. You need to protect yourself.*

I took a deep breath, turning back to look at her. She was so beautiful, as was Klaus, but Xi was also extremely psychic and she knew when there were things around. "What do you mean?"

The snake—it's latched into your energy. I can feel it because cats and snakes do not get along. The great lady Bast fights the serpent. At that Xi turned around and curled up, closing her eyes.

I headed out of the room, concerned. If the astral snake had gotten hold in me, I had to do something. Whether or not the doctor wanted me to go back to work, I needed to take care of this and finish it.

As I headed back to the table, I tried to think of how I was going to get around Killian on this. He wouldn't want me going, but neither could he take care of this for me. He couldn't jump onto the astral.

But *Hank* could. I returned to the party, waiting for the chance to excuse myself and call Hank. He would understand, and he owed me one. It was time to cash in my chip.

I SLIPPED AWAY FROM THE IMPROMPTU PARTY TO SLIP INTO the bathroom, taking my phone with me. After turning on the tap, I sat on the edge of the tub and called Hank.

"I need to take out that astral snake," I said. "It's got its fangs in my aura, and I'll bet you anything it's what caused the migraine. I still have a residual headache. The doctor doesn't want me to come back to work till next week, but who knows what will happen by then? I need to go over to that house tomorrow. And I need somebody who can fight on the astral realm."

"Well, I can. I also have a friend who can astral-shift. But January, do you really think you should do this? If the doctor says you need to rest, then why don't we wait until next week?"

"I have a premonition that something's going to happen before then. We took care of the curse. So that's off the table. But there's still something that doesn't set right. If we wait till next week, I'm going to end up regretting it. I can't tell Killian I'm going, because he's just going to want to protect me. But I also can't let it stop me from doing what I need to do."

"What if I tell Tad and we—"

"No," I said, stopping him. "Seriously, the fewer people we involve in this the better. Can you count on your friend?"

Hank paused, then finally said, "Absolutely. His name is Fifer. He works with demons."

"A demon slayer?" I asked. I hadn't met many of those.

"No, I didn't say he *fights* them. He *collects* them, if you want to know."

It was my turn to hesitate. Demon collectors could be extremely dangerous, and I had no clue how they slept at night because if the demons that they enslaved ever broke free, they'd wreak havoc on the collector. On the other hand, the guy would have experience in catching them and that was what we needed. And...there was the simple fact that I didn't know of any other way that we could eliminate that snake.

"How good is he?"

"*Good*. Just leave it at that. He's *really, really* good."

It was our only hope. That snake was far too deadly for us to take on ourselves, and short of burning the house down and salting the ground, I didn't see how we could manage to get the Shoners back into their home.

"All right. Can you take some time off tomorrow morning and bring him over? I'll make sure Killian goes to work. Say around eleven?"

"I'll see you then. I'll call you if he can't make it. But January, even with Fifer's help, this isn't going to be easy. And I'm pretty sure that Killian's going to be angry with you. Are you willing to take that chance?"

"Let me deal with that," I said, not sure exactly how I planned to do so. "I'll see you tomorrow at eleven. I'm staying at Killian's right now."

But as I hung up, in my heart I knew that I was going to have to tell Killian. I didn't want to, but Hank was right. If I kept it from him, it would drive a wedge between us, even if everything worked out all right. And that was the last thing I wanted to do.

THAT NIGHT THE DOCTOR CALLED AROUND EIGHT-THIRTY. "I know it's a little late, but I thought you'd want to know the minute I got the results," she said.

"What is it? Do I have a brain tumor?"

"No, I don't think you do. We can do an MRI if you want, but I wouldn't worry about that. There's no sign of anything to suggest it. Your hormones are off, however, and whether you know it or not you've entered perimenopause. That's early for someone who's of witchblood heritage. It doesn't mean you're aging any faster, it just means your body has decided it doesn't want to have children."

"That's actually a relief, because my heart doesn't want to have children either," I said. "Is there anything else? Should I be taking some sort of hormone therapy?"

She paused. "Actually, there is something else, and while it's not life-threatening, I think you should put me on speakerphone so both you and Killian can hear me."

Catching my breath, I stared at my phone. My inner alarms were screaming, and my headache was getting worse again. I looked up and caught Killian's gaze as he was clearing the table. "The doctor wants to talk to both of us."

Killian immediately dropped what he was doing and hurried over to sit beside me on the sofa. I put Dr. Fairsight on the speaker, and held the phone between us.

"All right, we're both listening."

"Have you heard of chronic migraine in humans?" Dr. Fairsight said.

"Yeah, isn't that where they have headaches over half the month?"

"Well, yes. Something like that. There's an equivalent to it among the witchblood, and it comes from underuse of magic. I'm afraid you show markers for it in your blood. Now, if you don't get it under control, then it can potentially burn out your ability to use any magic, and you'll be facing debilitating migraines at least fifteen days a month from now on."

I stared at the phone. "But I'm practicing with my magic—" I started to say, but the doctor cut me off again.

"No matter how much you practice, unless you've been actively casting spells and working with magic on a regular basis throughout most of your life, this can happen. And if you're one of those who never learned to work with magic on a regular basis, this condition begins to present itself around the time you're forty or fifty. You're prime for it. Since you're just now starting to use magic, it's been backed up and has sort of fried some of your psychic nervous system."

I looked up at Killian, letting out a small groan. "What if I start using my magic a lot more? What if I cast spells half the day?"

"I'm afraid it doesn't work that way. Magic is in your genetics. It's been dormant for years. I'm afraid that even if you start right now, you're still going to end up with chronic migraines caused by the frayed psychic nerves. You need to step up your magic to keep it under what control you can, but you have to be prepared. You're going to need to go on a stringent routine of magical use, and you're going to have to minimize stress levels."

I wanted to protest, I wanted to cry, but neither one happened. Instead, I sat there staring at the phone.

"Are you still there?" Dr. Fairsight asked.

Killian hastened to answer. "Yes, we are here. I think January's in a bit of shock. Was it just the lack of magical use that brought this on?"

"That's the major factor, but I believe that some recent trigger probably kicked it from a latent condition to an active condition. Honestly? It could have been the encounter with Mothman earlier this year. That's the best I can figure at this point. Whatever happened at that time, whatever he did to her during the time she still can't remember, may have scrambled her brain waves, so to speak."

"How many headaches…migraines…do you think I'll be facing?"

"It's hard to say, but anything from ten to twenty per month. They can last a day or longer. I'll drop over tomorrow about ten AM, and we'll go over everything."

That wasn't going to fit my schedule with Hank. "Can we make it the day after tomorrow? I have plans tomorrow afternoon."

"No, actually, that won't work. I'm on duty all day

Saturday and Sunday at the hospital. It has to be tomorrow or next week, and I really don't want to leave it until next week."

"Two o'clock will be fine," Killian said, answering for me. "We'll see you then. Thank you, Doctor." As Dr. Fairsight hung up, Killian turned to me. "What kind of plans do you have? This has been worrisome enough that if you are trying to change plans when your doctor needs to talk to you about a diagnosis, something else is going on. Out with it."

He was so stern that I almost burst into tears. "I was going to tell you but she called right then." I took a deep breath. "Hank and I are going over to the Shoners' house tomorrow and take care of that snake. He has a friend who can capture it. The guy's a demon hunter, only he collects them rather than kills them. The snake's still latched into my energy and I need to shake it off before it drains me."

Killian stared at me for a moment, his face turning white. Without a word he stood and began to clear the table. The tension was overwhelming. I wasn't sure what to do—whether to approach him and ask to talk about it, or whether to just leave it alone. But then I decided that, difficult or not, talking about it was better than ignoring it.

"*I said* I was going to tell you before going," I said, picking up a platter of burgers off the table that had gone uneaten. Killian pulled them out of my hand and pointed to the chair.

"*Sit down.* The doctor still wants you to rest." He paused, then shoved the platter back on the table and sat opposite me. "*Absolutely not!* You are *not* going to that house tomorrow. I know you want to finish a job that you started, but I *cannot* and *will not* put up with you harming yourself. You're going to end up hurt, and we'll all pay the price by having to help you."

His nostrils flared and he jumped up, grabbing the rest of the dishes and marching into the kitchen. I stayed seated as he brought back a soapy sponge and a paper towel and washed down the table and wiped a couple of crumbs off the floor. Then, still silent, he sat down again, staring at me as he waited for me to speak.

I tried to make him understand. "I think that the snake has got its hooks into me, and unless we destroy it or get rid of it, I'm not going to be able to dislodge it. I'm not strong enough and I don't think even Rowan is. *But Hank can help*, and Hank has a friend who can help."

"Fine. Hank has a friend who can help. Let them go. *You* don't need to be there. Quit trying to play Superwoman and fucking be who you are: A wonderful woman who has vulnerabilities and who apparently is entering into a time that's going to be extra difficult. If you plan on marrying me, I need you to face reality. And it doesn't matter whether it's the reality you would prefer. I'm not leaving you just because you've developed a health complication. I'd *never* do that, so if that's what you're thinking, get it out of your head now."

He was angry, all right. In fact, I'd never seen him quite so angry.

"Please, don't be mad. We have to get rid of this snake! Not just for my sake, but for the Shoners. I'm afraid that if I wait till next week it's going to be too late—"

"Fine. Let Hank and his friend take care of it. You *aren't* going there tomorrow. This is what marriage means: *We take care of each other*. I already think of you as my wife, because it's no longer just me and just you. It's *us,* together."

He stood and, before he headed for the kitchen again, he said, "If you run off with Hank tomorrow, we're done. I can handle a lot of things in a relationship, but I can't be with someone who won't take care of her own health needs, and who won't accept that she needs help sometimes. I'm not marrying Wonder Woman. I'm marrying January Jaxson. At least, I hope I am."

Before I could say anything, he headed for the stairs. "I'm sleeping upstairs tonight. You sleep in the guest room. And think about what I said. I don't make ultimatums lightly," he added, glancing over his shoulder. "I only make them when I'm desperate, and when the person I love is setting out to hurt herself. Don't test me, January. I may not be some alpha head of the Pack at this point, but I'm exactly who I told you I am. I thought that's what you loved about me."

In tears, I could only stammer out, "I *do* love you. And I love you for that reason. I just..." I couldn't finish the sentence because I realized I had no clue what I was trying to say.

"Sometimes you have to step back and let someone else shoulder the load. If you go with Hank tomorrow, then I'm going to walk away. Because as much as I love you, and as fiercely as I love you, I can't watch you self-destruct. Think... is it worth it? Because you need to let go, January. You can't fix every situation." And with that, he turned and continued walking up the stairs, and he didn't look back again.

CHAPTER EIGHTEEN

By two AM I was sitting up in bed, still unable to go to sleep. I hated arguing with Killian, and we'd never had a fight like this. We'd never been so close to breaking up before. Part of me wanted to call Tally and ask her if her brother was normally like this, but I wasn't about to interfere with her sleep. I thought about calling Ari, but again, I didn't want to wake up Meagan. And if I called Rowan, I knew she would tell me just to figure it out on my own. Finally, I picked up my phone and called the only person I could think of I could talk to in the middle of the night.

"Are you all right?" Teran asked, sounding sleepy as she came on the phone.

"Yeah, more or less. Listen, I'm sorry to call you at this time, but can you talk to me for a few minutes?" My voice was strained, I'd been crying so long.

"What's going on? Do I need to come over?"

"No, I'm all right. But Killian and I had a fight."

She was silent for a moment, then said, "What about?"

I told her everything, about Hank and going to the house and the snake, about Killian getting angry at me.

"I don't want to lose him. I was going to tell him because I knew he'd be angry if I didn't. Why is he so angry now? I wasn't just going to sneak off."

Teran surprised me. "January, don't screw this up. Frankly, if I were Killian, I'd be just as pissed. The doctor told you to stay home this week. She said that it could be dangerous for you to go to work. And the first thing you do is to make plans to take on a demon."

I was surprised by how resolute she sounded. "But I have to take care of it. I can't leave it until next week. The Shoners need their home back. And the energy is still hooked into my aura—"

"So what? Rowan and I will help out tomorrow. If it's not draining you, you can wait until next week. Or maybe listen to Killian and let Hank and his friend take care of it."

"But if I'm not there—"

"If you're not there, then what? Hank and his friend will have to do the work themselves? You'll have to give up control for a change? You won't have your fingers in the pie this time? I'm beginning to think you're addicted to the adrenaline, as much as you might deny it."

"*I can't let it beat me*," I said, the tears racing down my cheeks. "I can't knuckle under to this."

"We're not talking about the serpent, are we? We're talking about this diagnosis."

I shook my head. "How can I let myself be at the mercy of this? Maybe I can fight it—make it go away."

Teran let out a long sigh. "You think any of us wants to knuckle under to anything? I don't enjoy the fact that my knees hurt. I don't like counting my pennies before I go to the grocery store. *But I don't have a choice at this point.* I take what work I can get, and that means work that I can do without hurting myself. My knees constantly ache. You know why? I used to jog when I was younger. The doctor told me to stop because I was getting shin splints. Did I listen? *No.* I liked jogging. I liked keeping in shape that way. And now I'm paying the price. I didn't listen and I didn't accept my limitations, and look where it's gotten me."

I had expected Aunt Teran to be more sympathetic, and part of me felt like a little kid who had just realized the candy dish was empty.

"I guess I'm not used to giving up control. I had so little of it with Ellison that the thought of giving up control now terrifies me."

"There are some things we shouldn't give up control on. Our ethics, our way of life that we love, as long as we can sustain it. But honey, you're getting married. You and Killian are joining your lives together. *It's not just going to be you anymore.* It's going to be you and Killian, *together*. Yes, you're both separate entities and you'll remain so, but you have to forge a life together, and that means compromise."

I worried my lip. "I guess...you're right."

"What would you think if he decided to take off into the jungles with, oh, say Veterinarians Without Borders? To go treat wild lions on safari? What if he said, *I don't care that you're worried. This is something I have to do, and whether you like it or not, I'm going to do it.* How would you feel if he just decided to waltz into danger regardless of your feelings?"

I stared at the phone, part of me tempted to end the call. But I was only tempted because she had made her point loud and clear. "I guess I'd be angry. I'd feel like he was jeopardizing our relationship by putting himself in danger. And I really don't like the direction this conversation is going."

"The moral of my story is, sometimes you can't be the heroine. Sometimes you have to step back and let somebody else do the heavy lifting, because you know that you'll hurt yourself if you try. And that you'll scare somebody else if you go ahead with your plans. Taking on a demon when the doctor told you to stay home and stay out of it? Making plans before you consult your fiancé? You didn't include him in your life at all. And you're surprised he's upset?"

My tears began to dry. For the first time I understood why Killian was so upset. Not only was I endangering myself, but I was endangering our relationship.

"I guess you're right," I said. "I didn't think of it that way. Ellison tried to shut down everything I did, and I guess I thought Killian was doing the same thing. Or maybe I didn't think he was, but I was reacting as if he was." A noise startled me and I looked up.

There, at the door, stood Killian. His eyes were limpid, beautiful, and sad.

"I'll call you tomorrow," I said. "Thank you, Teran. I love you."

I put my phone on the nightstand. "How much did you hear?"

"Enough," Killian said. "I'll never stop you from doing what you love, unless I think that it's too dangerous. I'll never try to dampen your light, but I'll sure as hell try to save it. Do you believe me?" he asked, his voice breaking.

I nodded, tears trickling down my cheeks. "I believe you. And I'm sorry. I'm so sorry that I didn't put *us* first."

Killian was at my side in a second, gathering me in his arms. He kissed me, on my forehead, my cheeks, my lips, and my neck. I slid my arms around him, holding tight so he would never leave. He smelled wonderful, dusty and musky, and like apples and cinnamon. I sought his lips again, kissing him deeply as I straddled his lap.

"Never let me go. Make love to me and never stop. Show me I'm yours."

He fumbled under my nightgown, reaching for my breasts as he kissed me and lay me back.

As he slid under the covers, pushing my nightgown up, I

felt his head between my legs and before I could say a word, he was eating me out, loving me with every touch, every lick, every stroke. I held onto his head, bucking as I came hard, tears pouring down my cheeks as the emotion spent itself. And then, as his broad shoulders made their way up and he was suddenly hovering over me, I wrapped my legs around him as he thrust deep, piercing my core, and we made love until we couldn't move another inch, and then fell asleep in each other's arms.

THE NEXT MORNING, I CALLED HANK BEFORE HE COULD show up. "Listen, I can't go today. Do you think your friend can corral the demon without me?"

"He probably can. But don't you want to be there?" Hank sounded confused.

"The doctor told me to stay home this week, and I know why now. I'll explain when I come in next week. But my life is about to change and I'm not sure just what that means. I'm a little afraid, but I have to face my future and I have to accept what's happening."

"I don't like the way that sounds," Hank said. "Is there something we need to know?"

"Yes, but don't worry. I'm not terminal, don't worry about that. At least no more than anybody else is. We broke the curse, so that's a good thing. But something else has happened and it has to do with the headaches. I'm talking to the doctor this afternoon, but it's going to mean a shift in how I approach things. Please let me know when you catch the demon. Do you think you can make the snake let go of my aura?"

After a pause, Hank said, "When he catches it, the demon

won't be thinking about anything except how to get away. Fifer will break all bonds it has with everything else."

"What does he do with all the demons?" I asked, curiosity burning.

"Are you sure you want to know?"

"Maybe not, but tell me anyway."

"He sells them to the highest bidder," Hank said. "He's a broker on the black market."

I wasn't sure what to say to that. I didn't like the way it sounded, and I was pretty sure that it was something I shouldn't have pried into. But it was too late now.

"They're never used against anyone else. Trust me on that."

"I guess I have to," I said. "All right, text me when you've got it. Next week, I can take care of the other ghosts if they're still around. I guess that's it for now. I'll talk to you later, and thank you."

As I hung up, I realized there was a whole lot to Hank that I didn't know. I wasn't sure if Tad even knew, or what he would think about the conversation that we had just had. But for now, I set it on the back burner. As long as Hank's friend captured the demon, I'd be okay, and the Shoners would eventually have their house back. But I had a feeling that the subject would come up again at a later time, and I wasn't sure exactly how or where or to what end.

KILLIAN AND I SAT ON THE SOFA AS WE WAITED FOR THE doctor. Teran and Rowan had come over, along with Ari.

Teran said, "I'm planning my mother's funeral service for next week. There's nothing to bury or cremate, so it will be just a quiet service out in a park, I suppose. I'll let you know when." She shrugged, a sad look on her face.

"You know we'll be there," I said. "And I meant it. If Nonny actually left me her estate, I'm giving it to you. It's the only right thing to do. I still can't believe she wrote you out of her will like that."

"You don't have to, love—" Teran started to say, but I cut her off.

"Don't be ridiculous. We'll sort it out later, but I've already made my decision."

As the doorbell rang and Rowan went to answer, I tensed up.

"That must be the doctor," I said.

Ari took one of my hands as Killian held the other. Rowan returned with Dr. Fairsight behind her, offering her a place on the loveseat.

"Well, why don't you tell me everything." I stared at the doctor, wishing I could be anywhere but here. "By the way, the energy of the curse? It's gone. We solved that problem."

"I wish breaking the curse could solve this problem, too, but it's not so easy as that. All right, the name for this condition is energy reflux syndrome. There is a more technical name, but basically it's known by ERS. When a member of the witchblood heritage doesn't use their magic on a regular basis, especially during childhood, the circuits in the body and aura through which the magic runs get discombobulated. They short-circuit in a sense. It's like having a body that you never exercise. The tendons tighten up, the ligaments get tight, the blood doesn't flow as well, and you may even get nerve damage in some areas of the body. The same thing happens on a magical level."

Rowan let out a sigh. "I've heard of this. It's not very common. It happens sometimes among half breeds—someone who is half witchblood and doesn't know it, so never is taught to use their powers."

The doctor nodded. "If it's caught early enough, it can be

sorted out. But if it presents after, say, age thirty? There's no cure. You just have to learn to live with it, and begin exercising your magical muscles to keep it running as fluidly as possible. There are some varying symptoms that come with this. The first one that usually presents is chronic migraine. We're talking ten to fifteen migraine days a month."

"What other symptoms can present?" Killian asked.

The doctor gave him a faint smile. "Magic can go awry. Spells can backfire. So we recommend that people who have ERS stick to simple spells for the most part. There's nothing worse than a big spell going haywire. But magic *should* be performed every day, little acts. Casting wards, reading tarot —which is technically not an act of magic, but it uses the magical muscles. Meditation is another aid. Even mediumship will help sort the magic out in your body. But nothing will ever make it run as smoothly as it would have if you had been trained from childhood."

"Any other symptoms? Besides migraines and misfired magic?" I asked.

"Occasionally you might faint—the blood pressure can drop pretty drastically with this. You might develop allergies to certain herbs. There is a whole array of small things that can add up into a big ball of twine. I'll give you some literature about the subject and the name of a local support group. But your blood test pretty much confirms that you have it. And since you've already presented with your first migraine, I'd say there's no going back. We'll do our best to help you manage everything, but if the headaches start occurring too often, we're going to have to question your ability to drive. You have a familiar, correct?"

I nodded. "Xi, my calico, is my familiar."

"Unfortunately, she can't go out in public with you that easily. I suggest that we find you a service dog whom Xi can talk to. She can help you train the dog and be a go-between.

The dog can alert you as to when your migraines are coming on. Because the thing about these migraines is that they're debilitating. If you're driving, you may have only seconds to get off the road."

I stared at her, trying to fathom what this all meant for my life. "I don't know what to say. I literally have no words for this. I never expected this."

"If your mother and father had let you train, if they had sent you to the Aseer when you were young, this probably wouldn't be happening. Unfortunately, they set you up for a life of disability."

I sat back, staring at the coffee table. It wasn't the worst news in the world—it wasn't like the curse that would kill me when I was too young. But it was enough of a curse in itself.

"You should thank the gods that you aren't still with Ellison. Can you imagine how he would have acted if this had happened when you were married to him? And it probably would have come on a year or two sooner, given you couldn't practice *any* magic around him without making him angry." Ari shook her head. "Between your mother's paranoia and your ex's bigotry, they really fucked you over."

I stood and walked toward the window, staring out into the front yard. "Yes, but I suppose I don't blame my mother, not anymore. I'm convinced she was terrified that the curse would find me sooner if I practiced magic more often. Who knows, maybe she was right? Ellison... Yeah, he was an asshole. He's still an asshole." I pressed my forehead against the cool glass, staring out into the rain.

I was at a crossroads. One of those points where, depending on how I viewed the change, it would transform the rest of my life. The thought of having ERS scared me; there was no doubt about that. I prayed I wouldn't have to quit my job. I didn't want to change my life.

But all around me, life *was* changing. I was getting

married, and I was moving out of the house I'd grown up in. I had broken the curse that threatened to rob me of a future, and so—I had a future to actually face and figure out what I wanted to do with. However long it might be, I had the rest of my life and it wouldn't be cut short because of some angry lecher who lusted after my great-great-grandmother.

I turned around, looking at the four people who were most important to me in the world. Killian, my beloved. My grandmother Rowan who was a pillar of strength. Aunt Teran, who was a lot like a mother to me. And my best friend Ari, who would forever be my BFF.

They were here for the long haul. They were here, no matter what happened to me. They'd be here on the days when the headaches hit, on the days when I wanted to pound somebody into the ground. They'd be here on the days when I felt good, when I wanted to celebrate life.

Through the good and bad, they'd be at my side, and I'd be at theirs. Regardless of what happened over the next few months, I knew three things: One: I was marrying Killian, the love of my life. Two: I had people who cared about me, and who would stand with me. And three: Even if I *did* have a chronic illness, I no longer had a curse hanging over my head.

And those three things would make life more than bearable, even during the rough times.

I took a deep breath, and glanced at my phone as a text came in. It was from Hank.

CAUGHT THE SNAKE. ON ITS WAY TO A HANDY DANDY CAGE. SHOULD BE OUT OF YOUR AURA NOW. SEE YOU MONDAY. WE'LL BE TALKING TO MILLIE ABOUT THE GRAVEYARD THEN—WHILE WE CAN TAKE CARE OF THE GHOSTLY MATTERS, THERE'S A LOT OF OPEN QUESTIONS REGARDING THE BODIES OF THE MISSING PERSONS AND OF THAT CHILD. SHE SAID IT'S GOING TO TAKE AWHILE TO SORT OUT THINGS AND SHE MAY HAVE SOME QUESTIONS FOR US LATER ON. BUT

FIFER SAID THE BODY IN THE HOLE WAS LIKELY A SACRIFICE TO THE SNAKE—SO THAT'S A WHOLE DIFFERENT BALL OF WAX.

So, they had managed to capture the snake without me. I hadn't been a necessary part of the equation. I squashed the part of my ego who cringed at the thought and texted back, CONGRATULATIONS! I'LL SEE YOU MONDAY—IT LOOKS LIKE WE'LL HAVE A LOT TO SORT THROUGH AND WE CAN'T PUT THIS CASE TO BED YET.

Shoving the phone back in my pocket, I turned around. "I suppose I better ask Xi what kind of dog she can talk to. And I've made a decision," I said, suddenly aware that I knew what I wanted to do about another problem. "I'm looking for a new wedding dress. I've had enough of curses, and I'm not wearing a haunted wedding dress down the aisle."

Killian excused himself to bring out a bottle of champagne. "I'm not toasting the fact that you have this condition," he said. "But let's toast to a new beginning. You and Teran are free from your family curse, the first women in, what—a couple hundred years to be able to say that? I think that alone deserves a toast!"

Dr. Fairsight handed me the paperwork and excused herself to return to her practice. The rest of us sat in the living room and celebrated the future. At least, I thought, I had one, to make of what I wanted. And that was all anybody could ever hope for.

FOR MORE OF THE MOONSHADOW BAY SERIES:
January Jaxson returns to the quirky town of Moonshadow Bay after her husband dumps her and steals their business, and within days she's working for Conjure Ink, a paranormal investigations agency, and exploring the potential of her hot

new neighbor. Nine books (that includes this one) are currently available. You can preorder **Solstice Web** now! If you haven't read the other books in this series, begin with **Starlight Web**.

The Night Queen Series (steamy Urban Fantasy): Meet Lyrical, one of the Leannan Sidhe. A displaced princess, Lyrical is working for the newly revamped Wild Hunt Agency. Start with book 1: **Tattered Thorns**. You can preorder book 3 now: **Fractured Flowers**!

And a new witch is in town! Meet Elphyra, the sultry witch of Starlight Hollow. Together with her red dragonette—Mr. Fancypants—she both protects *and* heats up the town in every sense of the word. Preorder the first book, **Starlight Hollow**, now!

For all the rest of my current and finished series, check out my State of the Series page, and you can also check the Bibliography at the end of this book, or check out my website at **Galenorn.com** and be sure and sign up for my **newsletter** to receive news about all my new releases. Also, you're welcome to join my YouTube Channel community.

QUALITY CONTROL: This work has been professionally edited and proofread. If you encounter any typos or formatting issues ONLY, please contact me through my **website** so they may be corrected. Otherwise, know that this book is in my style and voice and editorial suggestions will not be entertained. Thank you.

PLAYLIST

I often listen to music when I write, and CURSED WEB is no exception. Here's the playlist for the book:

- **A Pale Horse Named Death:** Meet The Wolf
- **The Alan Parsons Project:** Breakdown; Can't Take It With You
- **Alanis Morissette:** Eight Easy Steps; You Oughta Know
- **Android Lust:** Here & Now
- **Animotion:** Obsession
- **AWOLNATION:** Sail
- **Band of Skulls:** I Know What I Am
- **Beck:** Farewell Ride; Emergency Exit
- **Billy Idol:** White Wedding
- **Black Angels:** Vikings; Holland
- **Blondie:** One Way Or Another
- **Blue Oyster Cult:** The Reaper
- **Broken Bells:** The Ghost Inside
- **Camouflage Nights:** (It Could Be) Love

PLAYLIST

- **Crazy Town:** Butterfly
- **Cypress Hill:** Insane In The Brain
- **David Bowie:** Without You; Cat People; China Girl
- **Dead Can Dance:** Yulunga; The Ubiquitous Mr. Lovegrove; Indus
- **Death Cab For Cutie:** I Will Possess Your Heart
- **Devon Cole:** Hey Cowboy
- **Dizzi:** Dizzi Jig; Dance Of The Unicorns
- **DJ Shah:** Mellomaniac
- **Don Henley:** Everybody Knows
- **Eastern Sun:** Beautiful Being
- **Faithless:** Addictive
- **FC Kahuna:** Hayling
- **Fleetwood Mac:** The Chain; Tusk
- **Foster The People:** Pumped Up Kicks
- **Garbage:** #1 Crush
- **Gary Numan:** The Gift; I Am Screaming; Intruder; Saints And Liars
- **Halsey:** Castle
- **House of Pain:** Jump Around
- **Imagine Dragons:** Natural
- **Julian Cope:** Charlotte Anne
- **Kevin Morby:** Beautiful Strangers
- **Lady Gaga:** 911; Paparazzi
- **Lorde:** Royals; Yellow Flicker Beat
- **Low:** Witches; Plastic Cup; Half-Light
- **Marconi Union:** First Light; Alone Together; Flying; Always Numb; Time Lapse; On Reflection; Broken Colours; Weightless; We Travel
- **Mark Lanegan:** The Gravedigger's Song; Riot In My House; Wedding Dress
- **Masked Wolf:** Astronaut In The Ocean

PLAYLIST

- **Matt Corby:** Breathe
- **Meditative Mind:** Hang Drum + Tabla Music For Yoga; Hang Drum + Water Drums—Positive Energy Music For Yoga
- **Miracle of Sound:** London Town; Valhalla Calling
- **Motherdrum:** Big Stomp
- **Nik Ammar:** Hollywood
- **Oingo Boingo:** Gratitude; Nothing Bad Ever Happens To Me
- **Pati Yang:** All That Is Thirst
- **Peter Gundry:** The Forest Queen; Autumn's Child; Heart Of The Forest; Lady Of The Dawn
- **Rachel Sage:** Among All Of God's Creatures
- **Robert Palmer:** Simply Irresistible
- **Robin Schulz:** Sugar
- **Rue du Soleil:** We Can Fly; Le Francaise; Wake Up Brother; Blues Du Soleil
- **Seth Glier:** The Next Right Thing
- **Shriekback:** Underwater Boys; And The Rain; The King In The Tree; Agony Box; This Big Hush; All About Nothing
- **Snow Patrol:** The Lightning Strike
- **St. Vincent:** Pay Your Way In Pain; Down And Out Downtown; Los Ageless
- **Suzanne Vega:** If You Were In My Movie; Solitude Standing
- **Tamaryn:** While You're Sleeping, I'm Dreaming; Violet's In A Pool
- **Toadies:** Possum Kingdom
- **Tom Petty:** Mary Jane's Last Dance
- **Trills:** Speak Loud
- **The Verve:** Bitter Sweet Symphony

- **Voxhaul Broadcast:** You Are The Wilderness
- **Wendy Rule:** Let The Wind Blow
- **Zayde Wølf:** Gladiator
- **Zero 7:** In The Waiting Line

BIOGRAPHY

New York Times, *Publishers Weekly*, and *USA Today* bestselling author Yasmine Galenorn writes urban fantasy and paranormal romance, and is the author of over one hundred books, including the Wild Hunt Series, the Fury Unbound Series, the Bewitching Bedlam Series, the Indigo Court Series, and the Otherworld Series, among others. She's also written nonfiction metaphysical books. She is the 2011 Career Achievement Award Winner in Urban Fantasy, given by RT Magazine. Yasmine has been in the Craft since 1980, is a shamanic witch and High Priestess. She describes her life as a blend of teacups and tattoos. She lives in Kirkland, WA, with her husband Samwise and their cats. Yasmine can be reached via her website at **Galenorn.com**. You can find all her links at her **LinkTree**.

Indie Releases Currently Available:

Moonshadow Bay Series:
   Starlight Web
   Midnight Web

Conjure Web
Harvest Web
Shadow Web
Weaver's Web
Crystal Web
Witch's Web
Cursed Web
Solstice Web

Night Queen Series:
    Tattered Thorns
    Shattered Spells
    Fractured Flowers

Starlight Hollow Series:
    Starlight Hollow

Magic Happens Series:
    Shadow Magic
    Charmed to Death

Hedge Dragon Series:
    The Poisoned Forest
    The Tangled Sky

The Wild Hunt Series:
    The Silver Stag
    Oak & Thorns
    Iron Bones
    A Shadow of Crows
    The Hallowed Hunt
    The Silver Mist
    Witching Hour
    Witching Bones

A Sacred Magic
The Eternal Return
Sun Broken
Witching Moon
Autumn's Bane
Witching Time
Hunter's Moon
Witching Fire
Veil of Stars
Antlered Crown

Lily Bound Series
   Souljacker

Chintz 'n China Series:
   Ghost of a Chance
   Legend of the Jade Dragon
   Murder Under a Mystic Moon
   A Harvest of Bones
   One Hex of a Wedding
   Holiday Spirits
   Well of Secrets
   Chintz 'n China Books, 1 – 3: Ghost of a Chance, Legend of the Jade Dragon, Murder Under A Mystic Moon
   Chintz 'n China Books, 4-6: A Harvest of Bones, One Hex of a Wedding, Holiday Spirits

Whisper Hollow Series:
   Autumn Thorns
   Shadow Silence
   The Phantom Queen

Bewitching Bedlam Series:

Bewitching Bedlam
Maudlin's Mayhem
Siren's Song
Witches Wild
Casting Curses
Demon's Delight
Bedlam Calling: A Bewitching Bedlam Anthology
Wish Factor (a prequel short story)
Blood Music (a prequel novella)
Blood Vengeance (a Bewitching Bedlam novella)
Tiger Tails (a Bewitching Bedlam novella)

Fury Unbound Series:
  Fury Rising
  Fury's Magic
  Fury Awakened
  Fury Calling
  Fury's Mantle

Indigo Court Series:
  Night Myst
  Night Veil
  Night Seeker
  Night Vision
  Night's End
  Night Shivers
  Indigo Court Books, 1-3: Night Myst, Night Veil, Night Seeker (Boxed Set)
  Indigo Court Books, 4-6: Night Vision, Night's End, Night Shivers (Boxed Set)

Otherworld Series:
  Moon Shimmers
  Harvest Song

Blood Bonds
Otherworld Tales: Volume 1
Otherworld Tales: Volume 2
For the rest of the Otherworld Series, see website at **Galenorn.com.**

Bath and Body Series (originally under the name India Ink):
    Scent to Her Grave
    A Blush With Death
    Glossed and Found

Misc. Short Stories/Anthologies:
    The Longest Night (A Pagan Romance Novella)

Magickal Nonfiction: A Witch's Guide Series.
    Embracing the Moon
    Tarot Journeys
    Totem Magick

Made in the USA
Monee, IL
07 March 2024